So this *was* p...
Allie thought,

It felt so good, so thrilling. Exciting and forbidden. She wanted to drown in the sensation. There wasn't anything wrong with a little kiss. Was there?

"I do have to admit there is something...different about you." Drew's gaze zeroed in on her mouth, and his lips covered hers.

The kiss was carnal from the first. Not rough, not aggressive, but hot. Burning hot. Wholly sexual.

Allie felt dizzy, having never experienced this kind of sensual passion.

Then his fingers pushed aside her underwear and Allie's world narrowed to his exquisite touch. He kissed her with a hunger, as if he, too, had lost all control.

Suddenly Drew stopped and lifted his head. His expression was puzzled and wary. "That wasn't supposed to happen."

But before Allie could utter a word, a strong-smelling cloth came down over her nose and mouth....

Blaze™

Dear Reader,

What if you found out that your sister was a secret agent and you had to take her place in a dangerous operation? That's what befalls my heroine Allie Carpenter. And my hero Drew Miller, the straight-as-an-arrow freelance operative who agrees to train her. Allie is sweet and flirty, and as unpredictable as they come! So please join the journey as these wonderful characters navigate a crazy, sexy road to their own true love.

And speaking of true love…Harlequin Books is sixty! Happy birthday! I remember when I discovered my first Silhouette Intimate Moments novel. It was like striking gold and it set me on the path to getting my first book published with Harlequin. What a thrill it was to see it happen. It was a dream come true. I'm still living that dream. Don't pinch me. I don't want to wake up.

Warmly,

Karen Anders

Up Close and Dangerously Sexy

KAREN ANDERS

HARLEQUIN®

TORONTO • NEW YORK • LONDON
AMSTERDAM • PARIS • SYDNEY • HAMBURG
STOCKHOLM • ATHENS • TOKYO • MILAN • MADRID
PRAGUE • WARSAW • BUDAPEST • AUCKLAND

Recycling programs
for this product may
not exist in your area.

ISBN-13: 978-0-373-79458-4
ISBN-10:   0-373-79458-4

UP CLOSE AND DANGEROUSLY SEXY

www.eHarlequin.com

Printed in U.S.A.

ABOUT THE AUTHOR

Karen Anders is a three-time National Readers' Choice Award finalist, and a *Romantic Times BOOKreviews* Reviewers' Choice finalist and has won the prestigious Holt Medallion. Two of her novels made the Waldenbooks bestseller list in 2003. Published since 1997, she currently writes sexy action-adventure romance for the Harlequin Blaze line. Karen is proud of her two daughters—one is already out in the world and the other is attending college. Although she misses the beautiful mountains of her home state of Vermont, Karen moved to northern Virginia in 1981 and then to Raleigh, North Carolina, in 2006. Her hobbies include watercolor painting and reading. To contact the author please write to her in care of Harlequin Books, 225 Duncan Mill Road, Don Mills, Ontario M3B 3K9, or visit www.karenanders.com.

Books by Karen Anders

HARLEQUIN BLAZE
   22—THE BARE FACTS
   43—HOT ON HER TAIL
   74—THE DIVA DIARIES
103—HERS TO TAKE
111—YOURS TO SEDUCE
119—MINE TO ENTICE
154—MANHANDLING
193—ALMOST NAKED, INC.
219—GIVE ME FEVER

To Diane Perkins for always being there
when I need her. You rock!

I'd like to thank Professor Gary Dill of
Self-Defense Systems, International for his
invaluable help on how to train the untrained.
All mistakes are mine.

1

HER SISTER forced her to commit a felony.

Allison Carpenter—Allie—bent down to pick her twin sister's lock, blocking the door with her body. It was a good thing she'd dated a locksmith, a relationship her sister had thought was rather a waste of Allie's time. But, lookee here—it came in quite handy. Besides, he was a fun guy.

"If we go to jail…" Jason warned. Jason Kyoto was Allie's assistant and today her partner in crime. He was Japanese and had one of those simply gorgeous faces, full lips, high cheekbones, smooth olive skin. His deep black hair streaked with red was long and full around his face and cut in a choppy style. With his simply dreamy almond-shaped eyes and a tight, well-muscled, broad-shouldered body it was no surprise women were unable to look away from him.

"Designing the perfect room is worth a little jail time. Although, if we get arrested, remind me to talk to the warden about those hideous orange jumpsuits. Orange just isn't a good color on me." She turned and flashed him an easy smile. "You know you're having fun. Who got me the lock picks?"

Jason rolled his eyes. "You're right. You suck me in every time, and I *do* have fun."

When Allie had mentioned to him that she needed to pick her sister's lock, Jason hadn't missed a beat. He'd shown up with the exact tools she'd needed. Allie didn't ask questions. Where a gay guy with an impeccable fashion sense had gotten lock picks was beyond Allie.

She'd solidified her plan the last time she'd visited her twin sister and faced the barren rooms. They'd had to sit on the floor, picnic-style, her sister lamenting about not having time to furnish her apartment, let alone decorate it.

Allie knew her sister was in sales, but it did seem strange to her that after all this time, her sister hadn't made time to buy at least a couch.

Allie operated her own design business, Allison Carpenter Designs, and had decided then that she would decorate the apartment for her sister on their birthday, but it had to remain a secret. Her sister had said she would be gone two full weeks and Allie expected her back today. Allie knew for sure because she'd talked to Callie last week.

She paused in her lock-picking when "the feeling" came over her. For a week now, she'd been getting this sense that all wasn't well with Callie. She'd tried to call her sister several times, but without any luck. Allie would have worried more, if it weren't for the fact that "the feeling" could mean anything from a bad-hair day to a break-up.

Actually, she should have had her sister's apartment done days ago. She was thankful for the huge job she'd started in LA for up-and-coming "It Girl," Lily Walden, daughter of U.S. Senator Marion Walden. An It Girl required a lot of attention, much more time than Allie had budgeted. Now Allie was going to have to work like mad to get everything done. But it would be worth it when Callie walked through the door and Allie yelled, "Surprise!"

Allie meant to talk her sister into giving her a key. It wasn't that Allie hadn't made the attempt in the past, but her sister's reluctance to hand out her key was strange, perhaps a throwback to the days when they had to share everything. Or maybe her sister was just being proprietary.

"Hurry up, Allie. I feel completely exposed here," Jason muttered at her right shoulder.

"Hi, Callie. Are you having a problem with your lock?" asked a pretty woman with dark chestnut hair.

"No, just dropped my keys," Allie said with a full smile. It had been fun in the past to pose as her sister. It was still fun.

"Hi, I'm Mandy," the brunette said to Jason.

Jason looked at her blankly until Allie nudged him.

"Oh, hi, doll. It's a pleasure. I'm sure."

He took Allie's cue to pull the girl aside while Allie did some more breaking and entering. She smiled when the lock clicked open and she entered the apartment.

Jason extricated himself from the young woman and followed Allie, closing the door behind him. "You have nerve, lady. I'll give you that," Jason said, taking a look around.

"That's me—nervy. Although, when I was teaching sky-diving, my mother called me flighty. Of course that was my third job in six months."

Jason laughed. "Flighty, Allie? That's lame."

"No comment from the peanut gallery, thanks. Let's get a move on." Allie smiled as he walked from the living room into the kitchen.

"You know that leaping before you look can be dangerous. Remember what happened when you tried to mix plaids with floral for Mrs. Jamison."

Allie winced. "That was an error in judgment, I'll agree.

But it turned out fine because the floral worked beautifully in her sunroom."

"You always seem to land on your feet." Jason examined the room and frowned. "This apartment sure needs to be done. Does your sister really live here?"

"Yes. She's a sales rep and is always on the go. She claims she doesn't have time to decorate."

"Perish the thought," Jason said wryly.

"Let's get started. We don't have time for chitchat."

Jason winked and pulled out his cell phone.

In a haze of waking, Allie heard the door close. Night had come and she realized she'd fallen asleep in Callie's bed. "Jason? Is that you?" she called.

"It has been some time since we've seen each other… your new lover?"

If Allie hadn't been reclining on the bed, she would have fallen to the floor. Yowza, this man was simply gorgeous! The last thing she'd expected after spending almost sixteen hours decorating her sister's apartment was a tall, dark and handsome man dressed in black jeans, black shirt and a leather jacket leaning impudently on the bedroom door frame, his eyes moving over her as though he knew her.

He probably did—her sister, that is.

Time to have a little innocent fun.

"Jason and I have been together for a while, but no one could replace you."

A lazy, seductive grin curved his lips. "I bet you say that to all the guys."

"How did you get in?" Allie asked.

"I knocked a couple of times and then tried the door. It

was open. We've been friends a long time. How is it that we never hooked up?"

His pose was all arrogant, self-assured male, like he had every right to be there. His thick, midnight-black hair was mussed, dark stubble lined his jaw, and his blue eyes were bright and seductive against all the sinful black he wore. His thumbs were hooked into the belt loops on his jeans, and his booted feet were crossed, giving the impression that he didn't have a care in the world.

"I don't know. Maybe you're not my type or I'm just not attracted to cocky, macho guys." She giggled inside. How long would it be before he realized she wasn't Callie? They had played this game at their prom and it'd taken their dates half the night to discover they had been duped.

He pushed off the doorjamb and sauntered over to the bed. "True, there wasn't much chemistry—then." He studied her. "There's something very different about you now. Something softer, more open. Have you changed your tough ways?"

"No. I'm just as tough as I ever was." Allie had to laugh at that, too. The toughest thing she'd done lately was demand more whipped cream on her mocha latte.

"You look great, by the way."

"I bet you say that to all the gals."

A fond, almost wistful smile softened his masculine features. Those blue eyes were like tractor beams, drawing her attention to him. Up to this point, this was merely a game to Allie, the how-long-can-I-fool-him game. But she couldn't look away. Her body grew very still. Her pulse picked up speed and, too late, warning bells went off inside her fogged brain. As had happened in the past, fun and games sometimes backfired. She should come clean right now. This look-before-she-leapt attitude is what got her in trouble.

She had to wonder why Callie had never told her about this guy. Maybe because he'd said they were just friends. Still, he was worth talking about.

But then he graced her with a bone-melting smile that kicked up her pulse yet another notch and drowned out her good intentions.

He leaned down and whispered in her ear, "Oh, babe, you're not at all like the other gals."

This close to him, she was overwhelmed by the latent power he exuded, could feel the raw eroticism of his hot mouth so close to her tingling flesh. Could feel her body respond instinctively to that intense awareness sizzling between them.

She opened her mouth to tell him she wasn't Callie. Smoothly, without warning, he slid on top of her with stealth and grace that left her almost as breathless as she'd been with his mouth near her skin.

So this was pure, unadulterated lust, she thought with amazement…and it felt so good, so thrilling and exciting and forbidden, she wanted to drown in the sensation.

Then his words registered. "I think, with chemistry, it's all about the mix," she said, giving him a very obscure clue that he wasn't dealing with her sister. In a heartbeat, everything changed. He would never know it wasn't Callie, and Allie could find out where these wonderful sensations would take her. There wasn't anything wrong with a kiss. Was there?

"I do have to admit, there is something…different about you." His eyes zeroed in on her mouth like a heat-seeking missile, and then they started to glaze over.

The kiss was carnal from the first. Not rough, not aggressive, but hot. Burning hot. Wholly sexual. Warm, soft lips meeting hers, open, inviting, offering. He traced his tongue slowly around the inner edge of her mouth, and then slipped his tongue deeper, probing and exploring. Allie tried to catch her breath and caught his instead, hot and flavored with the taste of cinnamon.

The heat flowed down over her, followed by the man's hands. He ran his palms over her arms, chasing shivers, setting off new ones, sliding lower. Desire swelled inside her, pushing aside sanity, blazing a trail for more instinctive responses. She arched against him, losing herself in the kiss, in the moment. She tangled her hands in the silken strands of his hair and slanted her mouth across his as needs lying dormant emerged. His hands slid underneath her buttocks, kneading, stroking. He caught the hem of her skirt, his big hand warm on her thigh.

Allie felt dizzy, as if she were tumbling through space.

Then his fingers pushed aside her underwear and Allie's world narrowed down to the exquisite sensation. He kissed her with hunger as if he, too, had lost all control.

He swore, low and breathless against her mouth, and when he tried to move his hand away, Allie protested.

She felt on the verge of spiraling apart, her body quaking with need and her inner muscles contracting. She heard herself whimper. Without thinking, she grabbed handfuls of his hair, arched into his skillful, decadent mouth and begged.

He teased that taut knot of nerves and Allie came on a shuddering, mind-bending orgasm that seemed to go on and on and on. The pleasure that shot through her was sharp and riveting and left her panting but amazingly far from sated.

He lifted his head and stared down into her eyes, puzzled and wary. "That wasn't supposed to happen."

Before Allie could utter a word, a sweet-smelling cloth came down over her nose and mouth. As her eyes dimmed, she thought she saw regret in the man's soulful eyes.

ALLIE CAME AWAKE slowly, as if it was one of those lazy Sunday mornings. There was a sickly sweet taste still in her mouth. Chloroform? The things she had done were coming back to her in bits and pieces, like a jumbled-up puzzle. She let them fall through her mind and lock into place, giving her the framework of what had happened.

She'd had an orgasm with a complete stranger, a man who was close to her sister.

With a start, she jerked to full wakefulness and found herself in a cold, sterile white room with one-way glass on one wall and a small metal table between her and the only door in the room. She closed her eyes and groaned since the light made her head ache. She opened them again, thinking it looked like an interrogation room. She shifted in her chair. Metal clanged against metal. She was handcuffed, both wrists behind her back.

This could not be good.

A wisp of panic worked its way into her like a slim, deadly stiletto. She shifted in the chair again, pulling at the handcuffs. There had been some kind of mistake. She'd only broken in to her sister's apartment, hardly a dangerous crime. Then the fog cleared in her brain. The man must have mistaken her for Callie. Was Callie in trouble?

If she told them she wasn't Callie, they would let her go. They *would* let her go, whoever "they" were. What kind of trouble was her sister in exactly? The wisp of panic became a large serrated knife.

She took a deep breath. There was no doubt in her mind that the man who was Callie's friend was a highly trained professional. But was he a cop or one of the bad guys? She shivered at the thought. She'd never been with a dangerous man and the thrill of it touched off vibrations inside her.

The truth had been in every move he'd made. She'd been too much into her game to see the warning signs. She must learn to listen to her head. She bet he was used to thinking fast on his feet, taking action and coming out on top.

Nevertheless, when they discovered the truth, they would let her go. She could take a cab back to her own apartment. Well, hell. She couldn't catch a cab. She had no purse, no credit card, no money, no identification. No keys to her apartment or business. No cell phone. No brains, too, since she'd gotten herself into such a fix, and had no clue as to what to do next.

Her sister would say that was typical of her.

Another Allie story to add to the ones already told at family gatherings. How did she get herself into these predicaments? They happened to her too frequently. It wasn't as if she sat around, thinking of ways she could get into trouble.

The door opened and the man who had seduced her with his eyes and that sensuous mouth walked into the room. Even in her precarious position, she couldn't help noticing the way his dark hair fell over his forehead, and her fingers twitched against the handcuffs as if to brush at it.

He was dressed totally different now. He wore a tight-fitting blue shirt with an empty gun holster strapped around his chest, outlining in relief his thick muscles, dark dress slacks that molded to his powerfully built thighs and shiny black shoes.

He was carrying a manila folder and he slammed it down on the small table between them.

"It's not nice to bug out on Watchdog, Callie. They're depending on you."

Allie was too dumbfounded to say a word.

At her silence, he continued, "Everyone has a price, Callie. What's the going rate for selling out your country these days?"

"Price?" Allie squeaked.

He came around the table and jerked the chair around. "Everyone has a price. What did he offer you to disappear?"

"Can I have something to drink? I'm really thirsty."

"No. The Callie I knew would die before she betrayed her country."

"I'm not Callie."

"And I'm Mickey Mouse."

"How's Minnie?"

He released the arms of the chair and turned away, but not before she saw the flash of amusement in his eyes.

"I'm Callie's sister. Her twin. I'm an interior designer. It's our birthday today. At least I think it still is today. Is it?"

"No. That was yesterday."

"Well, happy birthday to me. No cake, no ice cream. My present was to get kidnapped. Meanwhile, my sister gets an apartment makeover. I'd say it wasn't a very good deal. What I don't know is who you are."

"Did the chloroform addle your brain? You know who I am. Why decorate your decoy apartment?"

"Decoy apartment? Great. I've just busted my butt decorating an apartment that my sister doesn't even live in. The only people who'll get any benefit out of it are scary guys like you. And let's face it—you're probably not going to appreciate my butterscotch throw pillows."

He snorted. "Callie, this act isn't going to work."

"It's not an act, and I'm not Callie."

"Sure you're not," he said, but his tone sounded as if he wasn't quite sure. "And I'm not Drew. And you're not an operative working for a top-secret agency affiliated with Homeland Security called Watchdog. And you have no agreement to work for Watchdog in an undercover setup called Operation Meltdown as an arms dealer to broker a buy for a load of automatic weapons with the Ghost, one of the most notorious and elusive arms suppliers in the world. And we don't have plans to sting him here in LA in one week, and you won't be playing a crucial role. See, without you, babe, there can be no buy and no arrest."

He paused, but Allie didn't say a word. She was just too stunned to respond.

"This is all hard to believe, Callie. Watchdog was formed just about six months ago. You remember, because six months ago, you left the CIA to join Watchdog at the request of the President of the United States."

Allie swallowed. This was bad, worse than she'd first thought. She'd really stepped in it this time, her and her twin game. It explained everything—her sister's secrecy about her job, her barren apartment, her refusal to give Allie a key, her long business trips. Like their brother, Max, who'd joined the FBI, Callie had become a secret agent, the if-I-tell-you-I'll-have-to-kill-you kind. "Oh, damn, my sister is Sydney Bristow."

"What?"

"A government agent. And I'm not her. I swear. I'm her twin sister, Allie."

"That's good. Callie and Allie."

"It's true. Her real name is Carolyn and mine is Allison. It's our cutesy-twinsy nicknames. Is *twinsy* even a word?"

He shrugged.

"Anyway, we're identical twins. I'm not lying. I was in the wrong bed at the wrong time. You've totally kidnapped the wrong woman."

"I'm not fond of playing games," Drew said, once again placing his hands on either side of her chair. "Have you gone over to the other side?"

"Yes," Allie said, "I've gone over to the other side, all right."

Drew leaned in closer, his eyes narrowing.

"The Twilight Zone. Have you got Rod Serling out in the hall? Is he going to come in at any minute?"

He sighed. "I'm not amused, and the games have to stop."

Allie didn't flinch as she was sure he expected her to. "That's really interesting coming from some government spook who does that particular thing for a living."

"I'm not a spook. I don't work for the CIA."

"Who do you work for?"

"I work for myself. I'm a freelance operative hired to bring you in. Watchdog has strict orders about their agents, Callie. You neglected to call in at your designated time."

"If you're not affiliated with an agency, then that makes you a mercenary. They hired a mercenary to go after my sister? Why?"

"You know why, Callie."

"If I was Callie, I might, but I'm not. Why don't you enlighten me?"

"Okay, I'll play along. You haven't checked in to Watchdog for seventy-two hours."

"So, she's out past curfew?"

"Something like that."

"You have strict rules in the spying business, huh?"

"Look, you know as well as I do that all operatives must report in every seventy-two hours, especially when they're as deep under cover as you are."

"What exactly has my sister gotten herself into? What is Watchdog anyway?"

Drew gave her a long-suffering look, but Allie tilted her head, signaling she wasn't going to settle for anything less than a description.

"Watchdog was formed by the President of the United States as a branch of the office of Homeland Security. It employs a black-ops force to conduct undercover operations to apprehend persons of direct threat to the United States, to track and seize import of high-threat weapons, including weapons of mass destruction, missiles, automatic firearms and biological weapons, and to assist other agencies as needed."

"Then, pal, you'd better make sure that I sign something when I leave here because you've just told someone without a security clearance about a secret organization that she doesn't want to know about. I liked it much better when the only covert stuff I knew was written in my pretty pink diary. I'd much rather live vicariously through my ass-kicking heroines."

His expression never changed. Had Allie found herself

up against someone she couldn't charm? The man was good. Really good. He did this for a living, after all. He'd better be good at it. And speaking of good, the scent of him was intoxicating, and each time he leaned in like that, it only made her want to move forward, not back.

She leaned closer, whisper-close, so close she could feel the heat of his skin, see the unique golden rim of color around his irises. She lowered her voice, so that whoever was listening on the other side of that one-way glass couldn't hear. "Is that supposed to intimidate me? Considering what happened in my sister's bed, I have to tell you that you're only turning me on and your hands, they're very skilled."

"I was hired to bring you in for questioning, not... That was a lapse in judgment."

"That was a very powerful orgasm. It was wonderful."

"This is a serious matter, Callie," he said, but he moved away, glancing over his shoulder toward the glass.

"How many times do I have to tell you I'm not Callie? I'm sure you've pretended to be someone else in your line of work. I do it for fun. Twins do it all the time."

While he was checking out the situation, Allie's gaze drifted to the tousled length of his dark hair, the short dark lines of his eyebrows, to the hard, wide curve of his jaw. He was the ultimate American James Bond all wrapped up in a corded muscle-and-testosterone-honed-to-a-razor's-edge package. The only remotely soft-looking thing about him was the slight fullness of his lower lip. It fascinated her, the one provocative feature in a face that could easily have been described as tough.

And he'd kissed her and made her come.

She went to move her hands and the handcuffs jangled.

"Look, could you take these things off? I left my deadly martial arts moves in my other purse."

His eyes narrowed again. Geez, this guy needed to grow a sense of humor.

"I'm not dangerous." She crossed her legs. "The only concealed weapon I carry is my color wheel. I've never used it to kill a client, but, oh, I've wanted to use it like a ninja throwing star at times."

"Are you for real?"

The barb hurt and she stared straight at him. "Apparently you've never seen real before."

For the first time since he'd walked in the room, he reacted, his eyes widening slightly.

"Really, thank you for inviting me to this shindig, but it sucks. Can I go home now?"

Without a word, he pivoted on his heel and left the room.

This experience was certainly zooming to the top of her crazy list. Her family wouldn't believe it even if she told them. But, of course, she wouldn't. That would be just one more ditzy Allie story they could add to their arsenal.

"Is SHE Callie Carpenter?" Mark Murdock, Deputy Director of Watchdog folded his arms across his chest, a gesture that signaled he wasn't happy with the situation.

Had it only been forty-eight hours ago that Drew had been hired to track down Callie Carpenter and bring her in?

Drew Miller sighed. How could he have been so wrong? The moment he'd looked deep into those baby blues, he'd seen a vulnerability that Callie would never have revealed to anyone, even undercover. "No. She's not Callie. Let me see that file." Drew all but snatched the manila folder out of the hands of the agent standing next to Mark. "There's nothing here about her having a sister."

"Maybe it *is* Callie and she's playing us," Mark said.

"She looks like Callie and she pretended to be Callie. Twins do it all the time, she said."

"Where's Callie, then? We're in deep trouble here without her."

"Maybe you'd better try to find out?" Drew said.

DREW STOOD at the one-way glass in the small viewing room, staring at nothing. An hour had passed while Mark and the Keystone Cops tried to locate Callie. Drew had only worked with her on and off for years, and he remembered her to be very, very good at her job. His eyes rested on the face of Callie's agitated sister. For her sake, he hoped Callie wasn't dead.

The door to the viewing room opened and Mark stepped inside.

"She's in intensive care at Pitie-Salpetriere Hospital. She never left Paris. She was hit by a car three days ago while jogging. It took me some time to get information out of the French. We've sent agents to Paris to secure her and bring her home.

"Son of a bitch. She was protecting her sister. So typically Callie," Drew said.

"Callie's hard to read," Mark said. "But she's an amazing operative. While in Paris taking down French arms dealer Charles Girard, believed to be conspiring with a state-department official, she caught a break and was introduced to Jammer. He works for the Ghost. It's the first contact we've had with the Ghost's organization. Watchdog considers the Ghost one of the biggest threats to national security. We've been broadcasting for some time that Gina Callahan can get her hands on any kind of weapon. Jammer wants a boatload of AK-47 machine guns and Callie made a deal with him to deliver these guns to him in LA in one week. She related that much information to us when she checked in three days ago."

Mark moved next to Drew at the one-way glass. "She didn't go over to the other side like we thought. It could have been worse. She could have ended up in the morgue. We still have a shot at the Ghost."

"What's the bad news?"

"Callie has been injured. She has a severe concussion, causing disorientation after the accident. She didn't call because she didn't have a secure line and she didn't know who to trust. She's got soft-tissue damage and a broken wrist. Otherwise, she's okay. It could have been worse," Mark said. He rubbed at his temples and squeezed his eyes tightly shut.

Drew felt the same headache coming on. They'd had a word for this in the Rangers, but Drew kept it to himself as he turned, thinking about Allie's plea for him to remove the cuffs. He couldn't imagine what the unforgiving metal was doing to the tender skin of her soft wrists.

He also remembered how soft her mouth had been, the skin between her thighs, and the whisper of her breath as she tried to breathe around her growing orgasm.

Dammit. He should have known she wasn't Callie. Allie dressed like a modern-day Audrey Hepburn and Callie was much more edgy, that's why the Gina Callahan persona fit her so well.

He was trying to remain emotionally disengaged here,

but remembering Allie's reaction to his hands, his mouth and the pure, raw pleasure on her face didn't help. He prided himself on his cutthroat abilities. But when she'd crossed her legs in there, his eyes had riveted to the curve of silky thigh beneath the demure skirt she wore.

That was a first.

Getting a hard-on in interrogation.

Way to be professional.

He was absolutely positive this was a step down the road to disaster, a real shit-for-brains idea. He'd had no intention of touching Callie like that, but his attraction, his need for the woman on the bed had overwhelmed him. All she had done was given him the chance he'd wanted. He'd be lying if he said a small, yet totally irresponsible, part of him was hoping for more.

"I'd better get Ms. Carpenter out of those handcuffs, apologize and send her home."

"Wait just a minute. It's crunch time and I have an idea."

Drew didn't like the look in Mark's eyes as he stared at Allie through the glass. It was the look of a predator catching sight of its prey.

2

"SHE'S UNTRAINED."

"Even monkeys can be trained. She looks just like Callie. We don't have a choice. If you train her…"

"You hired me to capture Callie. We made no agreement about *her*. No way. I'm not putting Allie's life, my life and the lives of others at risk. Find someone else with a death wish."

Drew headed down the hall, his steps beating hard along with his heart.

"Miller!" Mark shouted.

Drew ignored him. It was suicide to put this woman undercover. He wanted no part of it. At least, the rational part of him wanted no part of it. As he walked, he couldn't seem to get the feel of her skin off his mind. The soft sounds she made; her warmth and zany sense of humor. Mark should just cut his losses and wait until Callie was well enough to continue with her undercover operation. There would be another chance at the Ghost.

He paused before a set of the glass doors to the FBI Headquarters, a high rise on Wilshire Boulevard called the Westwood Building. His rational and irrational parts fought with one another. Finally, he shoved one of the doors open and stepped out. Too dangerous. His interest in this woman was much too dangerous for him to take a chance. Distance had always served him well and in this instance, he needed to get far, far away.

"ME?" Allie gaped. "You want me to fill in for my sister?" The shock of being told that Callie was in a Paris hospital after being injured in a hit and run had not had time to wear off before she was being told that Watchdog wanted her to replace her sister. With nonchalance, the man had told Allie to call him Mark, as if they were study buddies.

"I'm not a secret agent. I decorate. Homes. Out in the open where everyone can see me. I use my own name. I wouldn't know the first thing about going undercover."

"We will give you a crash course in what you need to know. Leave that up to us."

The door to the interrogation room opened and her kidnapper stepped inside. Allie caught her breath at the sight of him. He always made her feel as if there wasn't enough oxygen in the room.

Mark turned and looked at Drew. "Changed your mind?"

"I still think it's an insane idea, but if it's going to happen, I want to run it." He turned to Allie. "I'm Drew Miller."

"Good…" Mark said.

"Wait, not so fast." Drew walked up to him. "I have demands." His hard profile brooked no opposition as his unblinking eyes met Mark's.

Mark stared at Drew and Allie got the feeling he was completely relieved that Drew had shown up.

"What are your demands?"

"I pick my team. I decide how to train her."

Again he didn't blink, just held Mark's stare. Drew's

eyes were fixed and unrelenting. A shiver of alarm raced down Allie's spine and almost stopped her heart cold. This was too damn real: her sister, her abduction, her in the middle of this crazy mess.

The sound of the door opening brought all eyes to it. A woman with an artful messy mop of auburn hair that looked as if she'd just rolled out of bed or stepped off a fashion shoot stepped through. Five feet eight inches of gloss and curves in a black pencil skirt, stark white lace shirt that clung to her and a vest decorated in multihued curlicues of the color wheel. And her shoes, Allie sighed with envy at the patent-leather Mary Jane Blahniks.

"Mark, give Drew what he wants, when he wants it, and in whatever capacity he wants it." Her voice was husky and melodious, but authoritative.

"Director Santiago," Mark said with reverence in his voice.

The woman looked at Allie with striking amber eyes. "She would have fooled even me, Drew. She's the spitting image of Callie."

"Gillian, where do you stash your gun in that getup?" Drew asked.

She smiled. "That's my little secret." She walked over to him and put her hand on his shoulder. "Why can't I convince you to work for me?"

"Then I couldn't tell you to go to hell right to your face."

She laughed. A soft, gorgeous sound that made Allie wish her laugh could garner the attention the men in the room were paying the stunning redhead.

"I hear that congratulations are in order. I hope to get to meet Mr. Santiago."

"*Esai.* I hope so. He's also out of the field and riding a desk like me. That's what we get for uncovering a major threat to the country." Gillian's face turned serious. "The President has made it quite clear to me that the Ghost is to be apprehended at all costs. When Watchdog was formed, the Ghost went on the most-wanted list. Now that he's vying for the position of Eduardo Fuentes's new arms dealer, anything we can do to disrupt Fuentes's operation is authorized. We're working on this in tandem with the DEA. Do you think this woman can do the job?"

"In the time frame you've given me…maybe."

Allie was used to skepticism, used to people dismissing her and not seeing her strengths. That was okay, she could deal with that. But at this moment, she was tired, her head hurt and she was being talked about as if she wasn't standing here.

This could be a grand adventure for her to expand herself, learn something new and help her sister and the government out. The danger part was daunting, but with trained professionals on her side she could do it. Just because this was a side of life she had never been exposed to nor had even thought about short of a movie thriller didn't mean she couldn't handle it.

She'd prove to her sister and to her family that she wasn't as ludicrous as they all thought she was. She could be as serious as her sister. All she had to do was put her mind to it. She wasn't without skills. Persuading a client to trust her with fuchsia in their house took talent. "I haven't yet agreed to do this," Allie piped in, rubbing at her wrists.

"You aren't even remotely qualified to do this. It's a suicide mission."

"Then why did you agree to train me?"

"Watchdog is going through with this plan with or without me. You might have half a chance at survival if I train you."

She hoped he was as good as Watchdog thought he was. She was completely out of her element. "I can understand why you don't have much faith in me."

"Faith has nothing to do with it. It has to do with skill and expertise. This isn't going to be as easy as matching chairs and a sofa."

She raised her chin and said, "That, actually, can be very difficult."

"But the furniture isn't trying to kill you," the director said.

"That's true. It's not."

"You're putting a civilian in danger and glossing it over like it's a walk in the park. I think if Allie is going to do this job, you should be straightforward with her about what she's getting herself into."

"Mark, Drew is right," Gillian said. "Drew, she's in your hands."

Drew turned to Allie. "All we're missing is your answer, Allie. But before you agree, I want to make sure you understand that this is very dangerous. Lose-your-life dangerous."

"Will you be with me every step of the way?"

"I will. I promise. Are you in or out?"

Her stomach knotted with tension. She thought about her sister's hard work, the stake the government had in the operation already, and the chance to make a difference. "I'm in."

"Do you require backup, Drew?" Gillian asked.

Without taking his unnerving gaze off her, he said, "Thad Michaels, Leila Mendez and Damian Frost. I'll also need the file on Gina Callahan, Callie's undercover persona and any other intel you deem useful." He finally turned his gaze away from her and Allie felt as if she'd been released from a choke-hold.

"Done." Gillian smiled. "One of these days, I'll convince you to work for Watchdog, Drew." She turned to Mark and said, "Keep me posted on the progress." Finally, she walked over to Allie and offered her a beautifully manicured hand.

Allie took it.

"Thank you for agreeing to help us, Allie. Your courage is admirable. You're in very good hands with Drew."

Allie smiled. She couldn't help it. But she didn't know *how* good his hands were.

Mark's handshake was a bit more brusque. "Welcome to Watchdog. We have a plane to catch back to Washington. Drew, keep us posted." They both left the room.

Allie's focus remained on Drew. This would be a chance to prove to herself and to everyone that she wasn't a screwup. She had a successful business, after all, even though her mother called it 'Allie's quaint interior-design whim.' They didn't trust that she would stick with it. She had Lily's place to finish, but she could multitask. A little secret-agent stuff here, a little design stuff there. It would work out.

Drew leaned back against the wall as if he didn't have a care in the world. Allie wasn't used to having her heart race just because a man looked at her, but she'd never had anybody look at her the way this undercover operative did.

It wouldn't be a smart move to get involved with him—even if the opportunity arose. That was crazy. She didn't know a thing about him, except that he was the complete opposite of everything she had ever known. A warrior. The real thing, a soldier who had put his life on the line for what he believed in. God, country—she wasn't sure.

She so wished with every ounce of her being that she could get on a plane and fly to France to be with her sister. But if Callie couldn't complete the mission for Watchdog because of her injuries, then the least Allie could do would be to help here where it seemed she was needed. It was ironic that Callie, the responsible one, risked her life and Allie, the impulsive one, did nothing more daring than combine colors.

Suddenly she felt weary, the effects of the chloroform and the fear sending fatigue throughout her whole body. She needed sleep.

Drew's hawkish gaze felt like a hard caress.

"What now?" she asked.

"Get you trained," his voice was clipped, every line of his body showing that he knew his work was cut out for him—to train her as an undercover operative to carry out the mission Watchdog needed done.

"Your skepticism doesn't help. You don't even know me."

"I know you. You go to work, pay your taxes and socialize with family and friends. You laugh, play and live. That's the bright side."

"And you're the dark?"

"There's always a flip side, Allie. I started my career in the military and I've been to Afghanistan and Iraq. I live on the dark side. And once you go there, there's no turning back."

"The dark side gives no quarter. Got it," Allie quipped as she turned toward the door. Maybe it was the fatigue or

the effects of the drug he'd used to send her into uncon-
sciousness, but her flippant words seemed to hang in the
dim, cold room, like a challenge.

There was no sound, no warning. One minute she was
moving, the next a steely arm wrapped around her waist.
Before she could even register the hold he had her in, he
pressed her up against the room's wall with his whole
body, immobilizing her.

"This is not a game, Allie." His voice was soft and grav-
elly, and very close to her ear, his breath blowing across
her skin as he spoke. "Your quips and off-the-cuff remarks
can't hide the fact that you're most definitely out of your
element."

Adrenaline washed into her veins on a river of both a
tiny bit of fear and a whole lot of excitement.

"You set me off with your forceful attitude." Allie
closed her eyes and took a breath in an attempt to stay
calm. He was starting to make her angry.

"You'd better develop a hard-hitting attitude, Allie." He
spoke so quietly and she had to strain to hear him. She focused on his breathing to slow down her own.

It wasn't going to happen. Not as long as her heart was
racing, totally at odds with the slow, steady beat of his. She
felt its cadence against her back. She was agitated, but he
wasn't. He was calm, holding her, but—she realized—not
crushing her, not hurting her. It was very effective, what
he was doing, and made pathetic the one self-defense class
she'd taken. He had immobilized her in one second flat.
Caught between his body and the wall was like being in a
warm, sexy vise. She felt the chill and the smoothness of
the paint against her palms, but against her back was heat
and plenty of it.

"You know, Drew, I've kinda had enough cloak and dagger for one day. I haven't eaten in twenty-four hours and it's close to midnight. You said something about food. As fun as this is, I'm wondering if fries come with the intimidation."

He didn't reply, but he moved, just enough to allow her to turn her head toward him. Adrenaline surged into her system again, only this time it didn't have anything to do with fear or intimidation. His face was so close to hers, his eyes translucent blue and deep-set beneath black lashes and the straight dark lines of his eyebrows. His hair was a bit long, increasing his sex appeal. He had a scar on his neck, faint against his deeply tanned skin, telling her that he wasn't kidding about walking on the dark side. His body was very hard against hers. She could feel the cool, steely ridge of his gun pressing at the base of her spine. Drew was now armed and dangerous. He was making her feel threatened on two levels. This mission she'd agreed to was, oh, so real and Drew was, oh, so irresistible.

A brief smile curved his mouth and his eyes closed for a fraction of a second as if he was trying to regain his control.

"You are the most exasperating…woman."

"My quotient for exasperating climbs when I'm really hungry. So, unless you want to get into my pants again, could you back up?"

"Get into your…" he trailed off.

"We're not going to pretend, are we?"

He slanted her a questioning glance. "Pretend?"

"As in the first time we met, when I melted all over you like warm chocolate."

He stepped away and she keenly felt his absence. She shivered.

"I thought you were Callie."

More cold water and this directly in her face. She winced and felt her face flush. A sickening knot of tension tightened in her stomach. Without anything to do with her hands, she rubbed at her wrists. "Is there a bathroom I could use?"

"Out the door and two doors to your right."

Allie walked past him and grabbed for the door handle.

"Allie," he said, but she ignored it and slipped out the door.

In the bathroom, she looked at herself in the mirror. Her blond hair was completely mussed, her makeup smeared and her eyes haunted with the knowledge that everyone seemed to compare her to her sister—perfect Callie who had chosen a profession and stuck with it.

Allie couldn't help wondering what she had gotten herself into.

HE'D HURT HER. She would have to bring up the orgasm. After that he couldn't seem to keep his mind on intimidating her. His sole purpose had been to scare her off but all he'd done was hurt her feelings by bringing up her sister.

It was a knee-jerk reaction. She threatened him and he knew it in his bones. Traveling from base to base as a child, tour of duty to tour of duty in the military, then mission to mission as a mercenary, Drew didn't owe allegiance to any one government agency. Drew hadn't wanted any ties. He tried to keep the people he worked with and for at arm's length. It was easier when he lost a colleague or had to move on, for him a familiar way of life.

If he compared her to Callie, it was Callie who was lacking. Allie with her soft mouth and her tart quips simply unseated him. He couldn't maintain his concentration when she looked at him with so much animation in her eyes. The promises were so tempting, so real. He thought he could almost feel them each time he got close to her.

Getting close to her was a dumb-ass move. But to provoke her he had to get physical. Her buoyant personality wouldn't be dampened by a few scowls.

She was spending way too much time in the bathroom. He slipped out the door and walked down the hall. Ducking into a darkened office, he retrieved her purse and then ducked back out. He approached the ladies' room. Glancing at his watch, he noted that fifteen minutes had passed. This late in the day, he was relatively sure that every female in the building would have already left. He pushed the door open and found her standing in front of the mirror, looking at herself.

"Allie?"

She jumped and turned around. "My makeup's a mess."

"I can see that. Here's your purse."

She smiled briefly and his heart slammed into his chest. Damn the woman. Anyone else and he'd be able to be as tough as she'd said he was.

"Thanks."

She opened the bag and took out a small packet and turned on the faucet. She pulled a wipe out of the small packet, sending the wipe into the stream of water and he watched as it lathered. With careful swipes, she took care of the mascara on her face. He stepped forward and pulled a paper towel out of the dispenser and slipped it into her hand.

"Thanks," she said softly.

He hadn't felt this bad in a long time. Why did this woman make him go weak?

Wiping her face, she threw both the wipe and the used towel in the trash.

"I can take you to your apartment so that you can pick up a few things. Not too much because we'll provide you with clothes and such for when you're undercover."

She nodded, rubbing at her wrists again and he could see the redness where the handcuffs had left their marks.

"Where are we going?" she asked.

"To a safe place."

She didn't respond. He could tell she was trying hard to control whatever emotion had caused her to pull in on herself.

His thoughtlessness made him feel like an ass.

"Hey," he said, moving a step closer and bending his head to better see her face. "Are you okay?"

She nodded, wrapping her arms around herself. "Yeah." The lie was barely a whisper. He saw it in the brief trembling of her shoulders, in the nervous swipe of her fingers that dislodged her silky hair, sending it down over her cheekbone. "Yeah. I'm fine. Thanks."

She faced the sink and picked up her purse. Her shoulder accidentally brushed against his chest, and the contact brought her to a sudden halt. Her head came up and their eyes met.

She was close, very close, all overheated woman and soft, sweet musk.

Tantalizing.

He found himself breathing deeper just to have more of her. *Stupid move coming up,* he thought. He was certifiable, trying to breathe her in—but, he loved the way she smelled. He didn't know what to make of the shadowed expression in her eyes.

"What's wrong?" He reached out and gently took hold of her upper arm.

She hesitated before answering, her gaze dropping. "Nothing. You said it all. I got the message. End of story."

That damn vulnerability. He would rather have her anger or her wariness. No. None of those were close to what he really wanted from her.

He slid his thumb along the edge of her wrist where the handcuff had done the most damage, feeling the silken softness of her skin.

"Agent Miller."

"Drew," he corrected her. He'd had his hand in a very intimate place last night. She should at least call him by his first name.

"Drew," she conceded, making a small dismissive gesture, part shrug, part turn of her hand—but he wasn't about to be dismissed, even though it should have been what he wanted. "This has been a crazy day—night—couple of days, I don't really know. Absolutely crazy and you haven't exactly made it better, except for making sure that I understand where you're coming from." She paused, her jaw tightening for an instant. "I just find it hard to believe that I'm going undercover with a man who neither trusts me nor wants me on the mission. The guy who's supposed to train me—" She stopped herself short and her hand came back up to cover her face. "I know I'm not Callie, but I'm not a weaker version of her, either."

He'd touched a raw nerve. Suddenly he got a glimpse into what it might be like being Allie Carpenter, getting lost in her sister's shadow.

"I only meant that I thought you were Callie because you were in her decoy apartment, on her bed. I was supposed to go there and bring her in, not…get her off. But I think I knew you weren't her from the moment I met you. By then…"

"What?"

"It was too late," he confirmed, bringing his hand up and smoothing his fingers along the curve of her jaw. He didn't mean to do it, but she pulled at him like a vortex. Before he could stop himself, he lowered his head and took her lips.

She let out a soft gasp, and her hand came up to press against his chest, warm and light. She might have been thinking of pushing him away, but she didn't do it. In fact, it only took about two seconds flat for her to tighten her grip and sigh into his mouth.

Dammit. He was right with her every step of the way. Her lips were as soft as they looked, the inside of her mouth even softer. It was a mind-blowing kiss.

He turned her deeper into the kiss, pressing her back against the sink. He hadn't expected such a pliant response, such surrender, and it went straight to his groin in a wave of pleasure so intense, he groaned.

Cupping the back of her head with his hand, he slowly increased his assault on her mouth, delving deeper with long, lazy strokes of his tongue and feeling her response in the subtle tightening of her body.

From the moment he'd met her he'd had the fantasy of this kind of kiss. But his fantasies were nothing compared to the reality of this full-out, hot-flesh-fused-to-hot-flesh kiss that made him want to keep her like this forever.

Big mistake.

If they hadn't been standing in a bathroom, he would have slid his hand up to her breast, knowing it would push them both closer to the edge. If it wasn't for the fact that he was supposed to be training her—and that didn't include his hand on her breast—he would definitely give in to the urge to pin her hips solidly against his, and he would have kept kissing her—kept kissing her until she was too hot to stop.

Just the thought of it made him hard.

He pulled away after that because he was moving onto dangerous ground. Okay, lethal ground. He was already on very shaky ground here. For a few seconds he didn't move a muscle, only tried to catch his breath, shift his thinking from south of his belt buckle to his empty head.

She didn't move, either. Instead, she stood still with her mouth on his, her breathing erratic, her body quivering.

She'd kissed him as if she was merging with him and they were becoming one. And once was not going to be enough. Not when everything he'd ever believed about being alone fragmented in the reality of holding her to him, with her inviting mouth hot on his.

The desire had surprised him, but he'd felt it as surely as he'd felt her tongue slide along the length of his, as surely as he'd felt her hand soft against his chest. He had a feeling that some of her illusions were being remade, too, her reaction to him as amazing and surprising as his was.

Gently, because he couldn't resist, he kissed her again. Brushing his mouth across hers in a light caress was a way to slow the moment when they had to move away from each other. To defuse the need to do more than meet mouth to mouth, he wanted desperately to have her.

Good idea in theory, but very hard to put in practice. One look at her flushed face and her moist mouth, the rise and fall of her breasts against his chest with every breath she took, made stepping back all the more difficult. Giving in to the temptation one more time, he dipped back down for another taste, then one more before he was actually able to let her go and retreat half a step.

Her eyes fluttered open, her gaze slowly clearing from a dreamy hue of wonder to an awestruck, what-just-hit-me blue. She stared at him, suddenly wide-eyed.

"Ohmigosh."

Yup, they were on the same page.

"We have to go," he insisted, his hand still stroking the back of her neck. "We can't stay here."

"No. Of course not," she said. But she was as transfixed as he, her pulse racing beneath his hand.

Somebody save him.

"I'm sorry." The words were out, husky and heartfelt, before he had time to think. It wasn't what he wanted to say. He wanted a room, a room with a bed and her naked on it. He wanted the rest of the night and into the morning. He wanted to know what turned her on and the chance to drive her out of her mind, just the chance.

Her expression told him he could do it. She would come undone for him, completely undone. It was a hell of a temptation, to take her and make her his.

"Thanks for saying that."

"I mean it." He slowed the movement of his thumb across her skin, his brows drawing together.

She gave her head a small shake and moved toward the door. Her voice strained, she said, "Well…uh, thanks… Well, I…uh, I'm really hungry."

He let her go. A sigh escaped him. Chasing her wasn't an option, nor was catching her—little Miss Carpenter with her smart mouth and completely wild kisses.

Nope. She was nothing like Callie.

3

WHO KNEW trouble came in such a wonderfully funny, intoxicating package?

Conveniently located close to the Westwood Building, Drew stretched out in one of the chairs in the loft where he stayed when in LA. He had a straight line of sight to the bed. He'd put Allie there after she passed out in his car from sheer exhaustion.

There were no interior walls, only wide-open spaces from one end of the loft to the other. It seemed that a view was everything in downtown LA, and he had too good a view of all five feet six inches of silky woman.

He couldn't really call the getup she was wearing sexy. It was classy and covered all the right places, yet the sight of her in the pretty eyelet nightgown made him wonder about the curves beneath the cotton. Especially when she moved around so much and he kept catching glimpses of her smooth skin. She sure was restless. She mumbled Callie's name a couple of times in a tone that indicated she was sure mad at her sister. But that was something Callie would have to deal with. His problem was the mission and how easily his composure had been shattered right from the moment he'd vowed he wouldn't train her or touch her. Right now he shouldn't even be looking at her.

He'd spent the night on the couch and had risen at eight o'clock when a knock on the door had revealed a courier with all the information he'd requested from Mark. With that information in his hand, he'd mapped out a game plan. Today they would start her training. He'd booked a conference room at the Westwood Building for one-thirty. This would give Mendez and Frost time to get to LA as they were both out of town at the moment.

He, Allie and his three team members would go over all that Allie would need to know, including her undercover persona, the mapped-out plan to sell the guns to the Ghost, a crash course on the gun-running business and a quick course in undercover operations. Then they'd go to the Watchdog training facility and teach Allie self-defense.

Pushing himself out of the chair, he headed across the living area to the kitchen to start a pot of coffee. He'd let Allie sleep for now.

He knew his breaking point and he was fast approaching it. Self-control was supposed to be his middle name. But she'd knocked him for a loop. No more, though. Not right now.

His cell rang and when he answered, Mark said, "We've been contacted through Gina Callahan's cell."

"By whom?"

"One of the Ghost's lackeys, a guy named Jammer."

"What does he want?"

"He wanted to speak to Gina, but the Watchdog operative now with her in Paris only said she wasn't available. He wanted to meet with her second in command. Guess who that is?"

"Where's the meet?"

"Starbucks at the Hyatt Regency in Century City in an hour."

"I'll be there. And, Mark—I need Gina's clothes and her cell."

"On the way to you as we speak. Drew, we're moving Callie to Walter Reed as soon as the arrangements are in place. I thought her sister would like to know that she's safe and getting the best medical care we can provide."

"I'll let Allie know. It'll be a load off her mind."

After he disconnected the call, he called Thad Michaels, big, tough Australian former boxer and con man with Special Forces training. He trusted Thad to watch over Allie. Thad was a mercenary with whom Drew had worked on many missions.

Fifteen minutes later he'd changed into a blue polo shirt, a pair of faded jeans and soft-soled shoes made for running and jumping.

Allie moaned in her sleep, saying Callie's name and then getting angry at her again. He walked over to the bed, thinking it was one more bad idea in a string of bad ideas that he'd had since deciding he was the only man on the planet who could train this woman for this mission. He knelt down next to the bed and reached out to brush the hair off her forehead. He looked down the length of her body. A damp sheen of sweat covered her skin, from the backs of her calves, in the tender hollows behind her knees, up her thighs, and over the incredible curves of her ass.

He wanted to consume her and not stop until he was sated. Instead, he stood up and shrugged into his shoulder holster and leather bomber jacket.

Drew checked his watch and looked at the door. What was taking Thad so long? He needed to get out of here. His gaze was drawn to Allie and again wandered up her body. He would never take advantage of her, but he was on a damn thin line as to whether or not he would try to seduce her.

Come on, Thad, he thought, checking his watch again.

He turned his attention back to Allie and noticed ink peeking out from the hem of the eyelet.

Perfect, he thought. The ink tantalized. His fingers itched to draw back the fabric to get the full glimpse of exactly what Allie Carpenter had tattooed on her shapely butt.

Hearing the rap on the door, he snapped the sheet up over her again.

"G'day, Captain," Thad said, when Drew opened the door.

"Thad, thanks for coming. This is Allie Carpenter, our new team member. She'll be posing as arms dealer Gina Callahan and I've requested that you become part of my team." He gestured at the lovely lump in the bed.

Thad eyed the woman, and then gave Drew a big grin. "Abso-bloody-lutely, Captain. You can count on me. I can keep her here, mate. As a matter of fact—" he leaned in for a closer look "—I think she's knackered."

"Yeah, she's out cold, all right. Fatigue and chloroform. Not a good combination for her."

"True blue, mate? Chloroform? Sounds like you had one bloody hell of a night."

"It's a long story, Thad. I'll have to fill you in later. For now, watch her."

"Got it."

"I have booked a conference room at the Westwood Building at one-thirty. Mendez and Frost are en route. I'll be back in about two hours."

"No worries, mate."

Drew had a lot of worries, least of all the beautiful

woman in the bed. He was about to tell Thad to keep his eyes off her when she let out a soft moan and rolled over, taking the sheet with her and effectively exposing her curves.

"Bugger me," Thad whispered, his eyes glued to the naked curve of her hip.

Drew went to Allie and untangled the sheet, his hand tingling from the combination of heat and silky skin. "Remember why you're here," Drew warned Thad. Smoothing the sheets, he then pushed the ends under the mattress to keep them secure. "It's better if you don't look."

Satisfied that he'd done all he could and that things would only get worse if he stayed, he straightened from the side of the bed.

She looked so sweet and innocent in that bed, her blond hair spread everywhere. He found Thad settled in a chair in the living room, watching TV. Thad was rock-solid. Honed as a commando into an elite combat weapon, he was trained to think two steps ahead of the enemy while under fire, underwater and outmanned. He'd scaled cliffs and rappelled out of helicopters, braved ice-cold water and death. There wasn't anything in LA Thad couldn't handle on his own, including the top government's elite and their amorous wives.

Nothing—least of all a 120-pound interior designer.

Checking to make sure he'd remembered to load his gun, Drew headed for the door.

LIKE AN APPARITION, the Ghost walked through the crowd; he was no specter but a flesh-and-blood man no one in his organization knew by sight. The trick was using the electronic gadgets he had at his disposal. One didn't need to be present anywhere when there were BlackBerrys, conference calls and the Internet—ah, he loved the digital era. Sure there were times when he had to be present, but concealing his identity hadn't been a problem. It was all about misdirection.

Even the savvy, suspicious people in the arms business were easy to fool when you knew how to fool them. That gave him a lot of pleasure.

It was so easy to get people to believe you about who you were. No one ever suspected that a lackey in his operation was actually the boss. When he told people the Ghost had sent him, people believed it.

And he stayed hidden in plain sight.

The Ghost liked to do his own look-see before he made any deals. Leaving the details to flunkies was a way to get yourself killed. It was his business and his life on the line and he intended to make sure both flourished.

When in LA, he often booked a room at the Hyatt. The lobby of the hotel was extremely busy with people checking in and out. He sat at a table waiting for Gina's man.

Recent rumors had brought him out of his opulent and extensive compound in Napa Valley, rumors that Gina Callahan had been killed in France.

Gina Callahan had a nasty reputation, the main reason he had steered clear of her when she'd first come on the international gun-running scene.

She was unpredictable, uninhibited, gorgeous—and as deadly as a snake. Versed in martial arts and weapons, she'd be a formidable foe. The Ghost had no intention of going blind into any deal with her.

He'd managed to stay out of her sights until the introduction he'd received in Charles Girard's hotel room only days ago when he'd seen her up close and personal. Everything he'd heard about her was true.

He was a man who'd been to hell and back and didn't easily let down his guard. But, with Gina, he'd gotten more than close to her. He hadn't expected it to happen, found it damned inconvenient.

Even now, he was still surprised that she didn't look anything like he had expected—older, harder-looking. She couldn't have been over five foot six or a hundred and twenty pounds. Her hair was black…and purple, cut short and spiky. Her eyelashes were sooty and thick giving her guarded eyes an exotic look.

And her eyes—he swallowed softly—her eyes were the clearest, most crystalline blue he'd ever seen, like a summer sky illuminated by pure sunlight.

He didn't believe in love at first sight, but something really unfortunate and extraordinary was happening to him. He'd faced weapons buyers and sellers who were some of the most heartless bastards on the planet. But something about Gina caused a meltdown somewhere around his heart.

After Charles had introduced them, he realized prematurely that she had extended her hand. Something people did when they first met. He reached out and slid his palm against hers. She had fine bones, a single silver bracelet with a heart around her delicate wrist. Her skin was soft, but he hadn't expected such a small hand to hold so much strength, her grip strong. His gaze returned to her face and—she was beautiful. Not pretty. Not cute, but freaking gorgeous, like a swimsuit-supermodel-fantasy woman every guy just hopes to meet in the flesh.

Braless.

His mouth went dry with the realization, and he had to

force his gaze back to her face—which was no hardship. She had a smear of chocolate on one cheek from the chocolate croissant she held in her hand. He had a serious urge to lick it off, but—damn—if his tongue ever got the chance to touch her skin, he could guarantee that he was going to lick more than her cheek.

"And you would be?" she prompted with just enough amusement in her voice to let him know how long he'd been staring at her like a silly fool.

"Jammer," he stammered.

"Jammer?" she said, his name sounding lazily silken on her tongue. "Do you jam people up?" One dark, winged brow arched in question.

"As charged," he managed.

"Where do you fit in the Ghost's hierarchy?"

"I take care of the negotiations."

Those deep blue eyes held his for a long, considering moment. "Hey, I heard that you're looking for some AK-47 automatics. That right?"

"You're well-informed."

"That's what keeps me in business, mister. Supply and demand. I have the supply, you have the demand. When and where do you need those delivered?"

"In two weeks in LA. What's the price?"

Gina named a price that he agreed to.

"So, the Ghost never does his own buys?"

"Not unless it's a large shipment like this one. He'll be there to seal the deal."

"I look forward to it."

She was simply mind-boggling in her tiny, torn pale-pink T-shirt and hot-pink, hip-hugging Lycra miniskirt. Not the run-of-the-mill arms dealer. It had never crossed his mind that purchasing the guns to resell for a tidy profit to Mexican drug kingpin Eduardo Fuentes would lead him to someone like Gina Callahan. It was his luck that two federal agents had severely damaged Fuentes's supply line to the U.S. The Ghost was ready to replace Fuentes's deceased arms dealer.

He cursed Gina now, thinking about how little time it had taken him to get her clothes off and slide deep into her. He'd spent three blissful days in her hotel room and they hadn't even gotten out of bed.

Now he was so deep, he didn't think he could get out.

Normally, he would have dissolved his agreement with Gina when he couldn't get her on the phone. But he needed this shipment and it was too late to put another one together on such short notice. He didn't like problems, but Gina wasn't a problem. He shouldn't let his emotions interfere, but he had to know she was all right. He had to see her. That's why he'd agreed to meet her second in command here at the Hyatt.

He hadn't prayed in a long time, but he prayed now that Gina Callahan wasn't dead as rumored. If she was, he intended to find out who had killed her.

He would make them wish they'd never been born.

JUST ON THE FRINGE of sleep was a time where wisps of thought wandered through the mind. The bed was perfect. The sheets were perfect. The pillow under her head was perfect.

Too bad it wasn't her bed. Holy cow! That's right! She was in Drew's bed.

She turned her nose deeper into the sheets. Oh, yeah, his bed, all right. The soft, warm blankets, Egyptian-cotton sheets, down pillows and the smell of him wrapped around her senses. From the angle of the sunlight streaming in through the windows, she figured it was about midmorning—and she'd woken up in a stranger's bed.

Oh, yeah, she'd agreed to take her sister's place in an undercover covert operation to apprehend a very scary gunrunner murderer, and she'd been too tired last night even to look at her surroundings.

She opened one eye a bare fraction of a slit. She could see all the way across the rather expansive room.

There was also a very large man with shaggy blond hair sitting in a chair. Allie bolted up.

"G'day sheila. Owyergoin?"

Sheila? Oh God, where was Drew? "Allie," she said. "Carpenter. Not. Sheila."

"What?"

"My name. It's Allie Carpenter. And you are?"

"Thad Michaels."

That told her absolutely nothing.

"How about a bit of tucker? There's bum nuts and mystery bag. I can put on the jug."

Oh, she finally got the accent—Australian. "Who exactly are you?"

"The captain told me to watch you."

"Captain? Captain who?"

"Drew."

"Yes, where is he?"

"He had to go out for a bit. He asked me to keep an eye on you. Sorry about the Aussie slang. I asked you if you'd like some breakfast. There's eggs and sausage. I can put the kettle on for tea."

Allie jumped at the thought of tea. "That would be wonderful. I should get cleaned up first and dressed."

"Right. It's the dunny for you. I can bring your suitcase for you."

"Thanks. I'm a little out of it first thing in the morning. Takes me a minute to wake up."

"She'll be apples once you get some tucker."

Thad Michaels was a big one as he filled the bathroom door with his broad shoulders. He set the case inside and came out.

Once inside the bathroom, Allie closed the door. Her stomach rumbled with hunger, so she had no intention of staying too long inside. The bathroom was huge, easily a quarter of the square space in the loft. There was a sunken tub situated in the corner with the shower overhead and numerous showerheads jutting from the wall. She sighed as she turned on the water.

After getting cleaned up and eating, she felt much better.

"How long will Drew be?" she asked.

"A couple of hours, I guess."

Allie heard a beeping from her purse. She rummaged through it and found her BlackBerry. Pressing the button, she brought up her calendar. When she saw that she had totally forgotten the meeting with Lily Walden, her "It Girl," she cried, "Oh, no."

Consulting her watch, she realized that she had just enough time. Lily's house in Beverly Hills wasn't far from Wilshire Boulevard.

This was the reason her family considered her scatterbrained. How could she have forgotten about her meeting? She saw that she had fourteen missed calls from

Jason. He must be frantic. She'd stop by the office first and then off to Lily's. Why, oh, why did she do these stupid things?

To her credit, she had been drugged, kidnapped and interrogated, and then recruited into a dangerous mission. So her mind had been on other things. She was supposed to have Lily's home finished for a party by Friday. Thankfully, she was almost done. She did some quick calculations. It was now Sunday, which left her five days. All she would need was maybe ten hours or so to finish.

"Problem?" Thad asked.

Thad would try to stop her. But she did have a business to run and she smiled. The bigger they are, the harder they fall.

DREW LET HIMSELF back into his loft. When he closed the door and turned around, no one was there. His meeting with Jammer had been productive. Jammer had wanted to know if Gina was going to be able to go through with the buy. Drew had told him that the buy was still on and Gina expected to deal directly with the Ghost. Jammer had nodded and told him that the Ghost would be there. Jammer insisted that he see Gina at a public place, one that would be safe for both of them. Drew said he would be in touch regarding Jammer's request.

The bathroom door was closed and for just a moment, he wondered what Thad and Allie were doing together in the bathroom.

His bed was made, the comforter smoothed down, the decorative pillows in place. He found some paper on the nightstand with a list:

1. Add color, too bland.
2. Turquoise would go nicely with the chocolate furniture.
3. Need a rug in the hall and a table.
4. Modern sculpture would work well, oh, that divine Kevin Sanders piece would be perfect. Talk to Drew about decorating all the Watchdog spaces. They need my help.

She had made notes…about the loft. Not only that, but she was thinking about taking Watchdog on as a client. He chuckled. He couldn't seem to help it. She was so unconventional. He went to the bathroom, opened the door and stopped dead.

The bathroom looked as if Thad had been wrestling crocs in it. The nightgown she'd been sleeping in was hung over the towel rack. He bent down and picked up a pair of silk briefs, rubbing the material against his thumb, thinking the fabric had been against her skin, against her clit. He was completely pathetic. He envied a swatch of fabric.

The bag she'd packed when he'd taken her to her apartment last night was open and his gaze got caught on other silky garments and unmentionables spilling out onto the tile floor. Unable to help himself, knowing he was violating her privacy, he picked up a soft bra, a plain white. He'd never thought of himself as a man who got off on women's undergarments, especially ones so white-bread, all-American-girl, but Allie was different, different in too many tempting ways.

A car started up on the street and brought him out of his sensual funk. They weren't here. Thad leaving without contacting him was puzzling, but if Thad deemed it necessary, he would have done so in a heartbeat.

He punched in Thad's cell number, but got his voice mail. Now Drew was starting to worry. He walked out of the bathroom and that's when he saw it, a note on the bar between the kitchen and the dining room.

He read the words:

Important decorating business. Will be back by noon. We should try that deli on the corner for lunch. Regards, Allie (aka Gina)

He pinched the bridge of his nose between his thumb and forefinger, caught between exasperation and amusement. The woman was a menace. He crumpled the note in his hand. Swearing, he flung the note toward the wastebasket and slammed out of the loft.

DREW CAME THROUGH her office door like a ramrod. Allie's receptionist actually rolled her chair away from him.

"May I help you?" she asked.

"Allie Carpenter," he growled in reply.

"Sh-she's not here."

"Where is she?"

"Katie, could you be a dear and run across the street and procure me a mocha latte."

Drew eyed the Asian man who sauntered out of a doorway. He had his face buried in the front page of the *Los Angeles Times* Home and Garden Section. He wore a cinnamon-colored silk shirt open at the throat with a loosely knotted Prada tie, a brown military-style jacket, tan slacks and really expensive shoes. His medium-length hair was jet-black, threaded through with bright-red highlights.

The receptionist stood. "Mr. Kyoto. This…ah…gentleman is here to see Ms. Carpenter."

"She's not here. Can I help you? I'm her assistant. Jason Kyoto."

Between Drew's military training and his mercenary pursuits, he'd honed his powers of observation. In his opinion, Jason was trying just a bit too hard to look the part of a designer. Then there was the slight bulge beneath the jacket, a sure indication of a concealed weapon. The kind of alertness that Jason was exhibiting signaled to Drew that Allie's assistant was more than he pretended to be. The fancy clothes couldn't hide the street tough beneath.

When he laid the paper down, Drew caught a glimpse of ink just below his collar. Anyone else would be fooled by him, but Drew was adept at looking below the surface and never taking anything at face value. Drew tried to calm his anger. It wouldn't help. "I need to find Allie. Could you tell me where she is?"

"She was here about an hour ago. She went to a job. I'm sure she'd be happy to help you when she gets back this afternoon."

Yup. Drew heard the steel that threaded through the man's voice. Not a trace of an accent, but Drew was sure Jason Kyoto was pure Japanese without a drop of American blood in him. "I'm afraid I can't wait." He smiled back with the same tight, controlled smile.

Jason's shoulders stiffened. "What's this about?"

"That would be none of your business," Drew told him in a clipped voice.

"Why don't we step into my office and we can discuss this. Katie, why don't you take a coffee break? And on your way back, get me that latte." Jason pulled a twenty out of his wallet.

Katie got up from her desk and couldn't get her coat on fast enough. She took the money from Jason's hand and exited the office. Jason moved toward his office door, and as Drew came in, Jason grabbed his wrist and swung Drew around, intending to slam him against the wall. But Drew was ready for him and in a smooth pivot, it was Jason who was plastered against the wall, his arm bent behind his back.

With a quick movement, Drew relieved him of his firearm. "A Fedor Tokarev, a semi-automatic pistol favored by the yakuza, if I'm not mistaken. A cheap, Russian-made piece of crap. I thought so."

"What did you think, hotshot?"

"You're no interior designer. You're a pro." Drew leaned into Jason, putting pressure on his trapped arm and wrist.

Jason grunted in pain. "Who are you?"

"Someone you don't want to mess with, junior."

Jason laughed. "You're going to tell me who you are and why you need to speak with Allie or you get nothing."

"Did *Callie* hire you?"

"Should have known you were a Fed."

Drew let him go, convinced the young man was Allie's bodyguard. Jason turned around, rubbing at his wrist where Drew had clasped him and held him to the wall.

"I'm not a Fed."

Jason smirked as only a youth can. "Right, you work for the government. Makes you a Fed in my book."

"And you, junior. Who do you work for?"

"You're a smart guy. Callie Carpenter, though this is the craziest thing she's ever asked me to do."

"What is that?"

"Pose as a gay interior designer." Jason flexed his wrist. "Whatever you've gotten Allie into, her sister won't like it. She pays me a lot of money to keep Allie safe."

No surprise there. Callie had been careful to leave off the fact that she had a twin. Her brother Max was listed, but he was FBI and obviously known to various authorities already. "So, it must have cheesed you that I kidnapped her right beneath your nose?"

"That was you? No, it wasn't pleasant to find her gone. I went out for pizza, but I left the apartment locked."

"We both know how easy it is to pick a lock."

"What could you possibly want with Allie? She's totally innocent and unaware of her sister's profession."

"Not anymore, and what I want with her is classified information. As I said before, it's none of your business."

"I'm afraid I'm making it my business, pal."

Drew made a calculated decision. Allie needed to be back in his protection. It wasn't wise for her to be free and running around the city where the Ghost was operating. He'd seen smaller things muck up an undercover operation. He handed Jason his gun. "Allie is doing a job for us…"

"What? Callie is going to be pissed."

"Callie's been hurt. She's safe now and being cared for."

The color drained out of Jason's face. "No wonder she didn't turn up the other night and I couldn't get a hold of her." He leaned back against the wall, stunned for a moment. Then his dark eyes met Drew's and he said in a steely soft voice, "Who?"

"We don't know. It could have been a simple accident, but we can't be sure."

Jason paused before saying, "I think I've got an idea who it might be."

"Who?"

"A notorious yakuza named Fudo Miyagi. If Allie is planning on taking on Callie's alias Gina Callahan…" He smirked when he saw Drew's expression. "Yeah, I know all about her and her mission to bag the Ghost. It's a good idea to get Allie someplace where we can keep an eye on her."

"We?"

"My guarding Allie has nothing to do with money."

"Callie called in a favor. Is that it?" Drew sat down on the edge of Jason's desk.

"She did."

"Sounds like you owe her big-time. But I already picked my team. People I trust."

"Tough, I owe Callie in a major way."

"Fine. But, I'm making no promises. Name's Drew Miller. Now take me to Allie."

4

JASON LED Drew to a huge mansion in Beverly Hills. Once they were through the gate, Jason got off his bike and walked right up to the house. "Shouldn't we knock?" Drew asked.

"Nope" was all Jason said as he walked into the grand foyer. The place was in different stages of design. Drew could hear Allie's voice coming from somewhere nearby.

"I don't think so. Move it over here. Hmm, no move it back."

"Bloody hell, sheila, make up your mind."

"Shh. I'm working. And thinking. Just move it like I told you to."

"A bossy sheila, too. How I let you talk me into this…"

Drew entered the room, which was lined with bookcases from ceiling to floor, with an ornate desk near a large bay window. But Drew's eyes were centered on Thad hefting a sofa. Well, a prissy thing that could be mistaken for a sofa. He had the piece tucked under his arm.

Allie sat sideways in a wingback chair, swinging her legs and surveying the area where Thad was standing. Neither of them saw him or Jason in the doorway.

"Look, this was supposed to take an hour. The captain doesn't like his orders bucked. He'll have my ass."

"Too late, Michaels."

"Bugger," Thad said as he boggled the sofa.

Allie shrieked, but Jason moved as quickly as lightning and caught the end before it tumbled out of Thad's grip.

Jason met Thad's eyes. "That's worth eight grand. You break it. You bought it."

"Eight thousand *dollars?* Bloody hell, you can't even lie down on it."

"You're not supposed to lie down on it, silly. It's a French Louis XV salon sofa. It's mid-nineteenth-century and it's upholstered with Aubusson tapestry in the theme of Aesop's fables. Oh, so chi-chi," Allie piped up, eyeing Drew.

"Forget the damn sofa," Drew ordered. Thad and Jason set the piece down.

"It's a damn pricey sofa," a female voice said behind Drew. "Mmm, Allie, you do have the most delicious helpers."

A tall, glamorous-looking woman in her late twenties strode into the room. Thad looked as though someone had just coldcocked him.

"You were moving this sofa around all by yourself?" the woman asked.

"Yes, ma'am."

"Oooh, an Australian accent." She held out her hand to Thad. "I'm…"

"Lily Walden, Senator Walden's daughter," Allie supplied.

Lily smiled and shook Thad's hand.

"Thad," Drew said between gritted teeth. The man was besotted.

Drew moved into the room and faced Lily. "I'm afraid this employee has an errand to run. Don't you, Michaels?"

"Errand?" he muttered.

"Yes, errand."

"I won't take up any more of your time. Allie, I just wanted to mention that I love the copper accents in the bathrooms. Nice touch."

"Thanks, Lily."

"The rest will be done in time for my party on Friday, right?"

Allie glanced at Drew anxiously. "Of course it will. Five days is plenty of time. I don't have much left to do."

"Good." Lily left the room.

Thad's eyes followed her out until they bumped into Drew's angry face. That seemed to snap him out of his fog. "She said it would take an hour."

"She snookered you. In the note, she said she'd be back by noon."

"Bloody hell." Thad gave Allie a hurt sidelong glance. She hadn't moved from the wing chair, but Jason went and stood next to her.

"I didn't want you to leave the loft. I didn't say I didn't want you to leave the loft, but you knew what I meant."

"Captain, I'm sorry. She has those blue eyes."

"You followed her like a puppy because she has blue eyes."

"Superhero-blue eyes like laser beams that take over a man's mind."

Drew rubbed at his temple; he knew exactly what Thad meant. Allie was irresistible, with her cute charm and those eyes that could drop-kick a man into the next time zone.

"Get out of here. I expect you at the briefing at thirteen-thirty."

"Yes, sir."

Drew walked over to Allie.

"The sofa wasn't delivered at the time the delivery company said it would be, and I had to find the correct place for it in the room, didn't I?"

He said nothing as he took her arm and pulled her up from the chair.

"Wow, you look mad. Are you mad?"

Drew still said nothing as he started to pull her toward the door.

"Okay, he's mad. Did anyone ever tell you that you look, like, überscary when you get mad? Mad-dog-killer scary."

Jason started to follow.

"Drew, I'm not finished here." Allie dug in her heels and since Drew had no intention of bruising her arm, he stopped.

"We don't have time for decorating, Allie."

"Don't say it like that. It's my job. My livelihood. I've already accepted a retainer from Lily. She's an 'It Girl,' Drew. Do you know what this will do for my business?"

"Do you remember Watchdog and what you have already agreed to, Allie? I didn't twist your arm."

"No, that is true. You didn't. Wait, please." Her resistance pulled him to another stop.

"Let me explain," she continued. "This is the kind of thing that I do. I leap before I look. Truly. Ask my family if you don't believe me," she said bitterly. "I'm not proud of it. I'm quirky like that, but I do want to go through with everything. I just need a few more minutes here. Don't we have time?"

"Our time is going to quickly run out. I've gleaned some important information that you need to be briefed on." Drew looked at Jason. "And your assistant here has something he also needs to tell you."

"A second. I only need a second." It was then that she

looked at him with those blue eyes, so expressive, so deep he could get lost in them.

"Jason," he said wearily. "Help me move this."

Jason dutifully bent down and grabbed one end of the sofa.

It was bad enough that he caved about the damn sofa, but she also got him and Jason to hang a tapestry.

"Now the throw pillows and we're—"

"I draw the line at throw pillows, Allie. It's time to go."

"All right," she said in that scolding, narrow-eyed way that still made her look cute. She was probably trying to be a jungle cat, but was only turning out to be a little spitting kitten. He was skeptical that she could pull off the Gina Callahan persona.

They were all going to die.

She picked up the gold and brown pillows and set them on the sofa.

He walked out of the room that was shaping up into a fancy library and flipped open his phone. He punched in the phone number and waited for the call to go through.

"Yeah," Damian Frost's cool Irish accent was evident in his low voice coming through the phone. In the unofficial covert-ops business, he was known as a shadow warrior: unconventional, with long dark hair held in a ponytail, enigmatic, a man of very few words and deadly actions. Drew would have called him a global vigilante except for his dedication to his own rigid code of conduct and his ability to carry out missions with almost no violence. Reported to have once been part of the IRA, he had devoted his life to busting arms dealers, also he was the most amazing info-gathering hacker Drew had ever met.

"I need you to check someone out for me."

"Shoot."

"Kyoto—goes by the name Jason Kyoto. I think he is, or was, yakuza. I saw a tattoo just below his collarbone. I'd stake my life he's full Japanese, but he speaks English like he was born and raised here. I want to know what he eats for lunch, Frost."

"You got it. I'll see you at one-thirty."

Drew checked on Allie who was now in deep discussion with Jason. Drew didn't have to guess what they were talking about. Her expression was one of utter betrayal. Allie looked pale and shaken.

Her blue eyes got brighter and Drew felt something, very near to where his heart might be, turn over. He resented Kyoto. He resented that this news made Allie look as if she didn't know who she was or where to turn. He should be worrying about how it would affect her role-playing and her effectiveness in the mission at hand. He was her trainer. He was a fool to think that he could be her harbor, her rock. Yet, that was exactly what he wanted to be.

She turned away from Jason and met Drew's eyes, looking very much like a woman whose world had crumbled.

He called to her. "Allie, let's go. Now."

The autocratic tone stiffened her spine and dried her tears, just as he had hoped it would. She marched across the room and out the door. Drew could almost feel sorry for Jason as he watched her go with his heart in his eyes. It was obvious to Drew that Jason cared about Allie. Interesting. What did a possible former yakuza know about caring and decency? The kid was a mystery and Drew did not like mysteries, especially where Allie was concerned.

He jerked his head when Jason looked at him and the kid followed them out.

"Are you okay?" Drew asked Allie after he'd gotten into the driver's seat of his car and closed the door. Jason followed them out and straddled a sleek red motorcycle right behind Drew's car. She realized that he had no intention of letting her out of his sight.

Breathe or faint, Allie told herself, knowing it had to be one or the other. She was trembling inside, which she hated, and she couldn't seem to get her mind around what Jason had just told her in Lily Walden's library.

Drew drove back to the loft since it was nearly noon. After parking, he led Allie, with Jason trailing, to the deli Allie had mentioned in her note to grab some sandwiches before the meeting with Damian and Leila. The Westwood Building was within walking distance.

"Why is he here, Drew?"

"He's your bodyguard, Allie. You tell me."

"He answered an ad in the paper. One my sister convinced me to put in. She said I worked too hard. I really needed an assistant. I didn't know he'd come with a gun strapped to his chest and lies on his lips."

"Allie, Callie just wants to keep you safe," Jason said as calmly and serenely as if he were channeling the Dalai Lama.

"I trusted you. I thought you were a gay designer. Come to find out you're a straight bodyguard. One my secret-agent sister hired. Man, this sounds like some freaking movie."

"You don't have to do this," Jason said.

She could barely look at Jason's face and the naked pain in his eyes.

"Yes, I do," she said, as she collapsed into a booth isolated from the lunch crowd. She let out a breath she'd accidentally held. She wasn't going to walk away from this mess and leave him to handle it. She wasn't going to walk away from him, no matter what. This was one job she was going to see through to the end.

It hurt that her sister hadn't confided in her. Hadn't trusted her enough to tell her about Jason, to be honest with her. And Jason…he'd betrayed her. Even looking at him now, she was feeling stupid. How could she have missed his street-wise eyes, his hard, honed body, the way he held himself? Just like Drew. He said he was a ninja and she'd never even seen it. Oh, it was all so overwhelming. But as awful as Jason's betrayal was, it was nothing compared to the trouble she was in, right now between her pseudo-secret-agent status and Drew Miller's sex appeal.

One look at him and a hundred other memories came flooding back. He'd slowly, methodically brought her to orgasm before she'd even known his name. When he'd kissed her in a bathroom downtown, she'd melted with pleasure and need. Absolutely melted.

Her gaze dropped to his mouth, and her blush grew even hotter. No man had ever kissed her like Drew Miller—long and slow and wet, and deep, as though his next breath depended on her kiss. His mouth fitted hers as if they were made for each other. His body was so strong and hard up against her, moving against her. She could have kissed him forever.

Drew said, "Why don't you give her some time? We have a lot to get to today."

The sheer concern in his voice startled her out of her reverie, and with effort, she forced herself to meet his eyes again. He looked lethal with his tough-guy clothes, tousled hair and beard-shadowed jaw, and he obviously needed a reality check on one of the less-pleasant facts of life, one she would have thought he'd known.

"I can't leave her. I've already lost her once."

The sheer self-condemnation in Jason's voice cut into her. She almost rose and put her arms around him to comfort him. This was all so real, so not fun. Allie preferred her life to be uncomplicated and easy. That had all changed now that Drew had stepped into her life and she'd agreed to an alias.

"I'll take care of her. I give you my word."

The sound of Drew's voice made her shiver inside. Hot mouth, even hotter hands all over her. The heated memory wouldn't go away. From the moment she'd woken to find a huge, gorgeous Aussie bodyguard in the loft to now, that one memory of their kiss had set her pulse pounding.

Too bad he'd pulled away. Too bad he'd gone all secret-agent-in-charge on her again. She wondered what his story was. What kept him from taking what he wanted with her? She couldn't quite understand.

She had every intention of working on the problem until she did.

They ate in silence. When the meal was done, Drew took Jason aside and talked to him quietly. Allie waited at the table.

Jason gave her one more glance, but she couldn't meet his eyes. Not now. She turned away until he left. Her sister and now Jason. It was too much to take in. Kidnapped, bamboozled into becoming Gina Callahan by a slick government agent and finding herself thoroughly intrigued by a very dangerous man was more than one person could handle in such a short time-span.

It was easy to let all these concerns overshadow the one emotion she didn't want to feel.

Fear.

Why had Callie felt it necessary to hire a bodyguard for her? Who was after Callie and why did it make Allie a target that needed protecting? Was Callie in the hospital because someone had tried to kill her? What if it wasn't an accident as Watchdog thought?

"The meeting starts in fifteen minutes. Let's get going."

They walked in silence to the Westwood Building. It was convenient that the loft was so nearby. Once inside, they obtained their visitor's badges and proceeded to the conference room.

When they entered, it was empty, the other members expected in about ten minutes.

"Have you heard anything about how my sister is doing? I don't even know who to call to get updates," Allie said.

"There's no change. Mark told me she's being moved to Walter Reed. Anytime you want to know about Callie, ask and I'll find out for you."

"I'm so worried about her. I really want to be there for her." She loved the way his eyes softened. It made her feel warm inside.

"Of course you do. It's only natural."

He pulled Allie into his arms. She went because she was feeling, oh, so lost with everything that was happening to her. "It's just that we've never had secrets between us before. At least, I thought we hadn't." Her words were muffled with her face pressed to his chest.

"This business requires secrets. It's how we do the job."

His hand smoothed through her hair and it felt so good Allie had to wonder if this was the way he treated her sister. The question just popped out of her stupid mouth.

"How close were you with my sister?"

He stiffened against her and moved away. "Like I told you before, the chemistry just wasn't there. We're more like brother and sister."

"She's more your type."

"How do you know what my type is, Allie? You don't know me."

"I know some things about you. I know that you care about your country and you do your best to protect its citizens. You're dedicated and skilled. And your lips are so soft. I have to confess that I can't get that kiss out of my mind, Drew. I want more."

"I don't think that's a good idea."

"No. It probably isn't a good idea, but I'm not known for my good ideas. Am I?"

"You're settled in LA. You have a business and friends. I'm nothing like that, Allie. I go where jobs are and face danger every day. Getting involved with me is a bad decision. I'm here today, gone tomorrow."

"So?"

"So you're not Callie, even though you pretend to be."

She turned away.

"Allie, wait… I didn't mean—"

"I know what you meant. Wacky Allie. Can't remember important meetings. Goes off on a tangent. Doesn't have a freaking clue she has a ninja bodyguard. But she does have skills. She can force scary secret agents into moving around furniture."

Drew chuckled. He couldn't help it. The memory of Thad dragging that tiny sofa around while Allie directed him was priceless.

"What's so funny?"

"You are."

She came closer to him warily. "I think you like that about me."

"I like way too much about you."

She reached up and touched his lips with her fingertips, knowing her own mouth was one of the most sensitive places on her body. She wanted to feel him, drink him in through her skin.

She held his dark-eyed gaze and heat coiled low in her belly.

She pressed on his mouth with her thumb, a slow, hot glide across his soft, made-for-kissing mouth. "Don't make me beg."

She hadn't expected that drowning would feel so delicious. But she was drowning. Drowning in desire and confusion—and desire kept winning, every second, every heartbeat.

"Beg, just a few words, Allie."

"Please, Drew. Kiss me. I want it so…"

She didn't finish her sentence as the word *much* got muffled. Slanting his lips across hers, he sought entrance with his tongue. She responded immediately with a gasp of pleasure, and he took the kiss home, slipping inside and giving her a piece of heaven.

The danger of what she'd decided to do seemed to hit her with a force that was felt. The realization added a dark thrill to the whole heart-stopping experience of having Drew make love to her mouth. She didn't know what else to call what he was doing. It was more than a kiss, more than any kiss she'd ever been given. The slow, deliberate sucking on her tongue was meant without a doubt to make her think of a far more intimate act.

And she was—shameless. The feel of him in her mouth, the taste of him, was intoxicating, dizzying. He set her on fire with his kiss. Every inch of her wanted more. It was crazy. Crazy and hot and utterly sexual in a way she'd thought she would never know except in her fantasies— but the reality of it was much more intense, the silkiness of his hair sliding through her fingers, the rough edge of his jaw beneath her palm, the strength of his arms wrapped around her. In her fantasies, everything was safe. She was in charge. With him, nothing was safe. The pure physical energy of him was a force to be reckoned with. He was powerful, dangerous and unpredictably seductive. She didn't know what was going to happen next....

Drew pulled away and swore vehemently. She wasn't sure if it was because he'd succumbed to the craziness that was going on between them or because they had to stop.

The door to the conference room opened and a man stepped through, and Allie felt an instinctual need to be extremely careful. Of all the operatives she'd met up until now, including Drew, only this one made her feel almost as if someone had let a tiger loose in the room.

He was tall and well-built. His dark hair was pulled severely back off a very handsome face, almost unbelievably handsome. His black eyes were alert and full of warnings.

Allie suddenly felt a need to flee.

"We've got trouble," the man said.

Drew scrubbed at his face. "Tell me something I don't know," he said, looking at Allie.

Allie wanted to shrink into an insignificant spot on the floor. For the first time since this roller-coaster ride had started, she wished she'd never heard about Watchdog.

She wished that her sister was simply a buyer for Neiman Marcus, and that she herself could go there right now and treat herself to a pair of the most expensive shoes she could find—and be normal.

5

"YOU LOOK just like your sister," Frost said. He had a secretive expression and world-weary eyes.

Allie swallowed and tried to smile, but it felt unnatural on her face.

Locking those scary eyes on her, Frost set down a garment bag, a suitcase and a laptop. He went to a table in the front of the room and hooked up the computer. He then sat down in one of the conference-room chairs. Thad and Leila arrived shortly after Damian. Leila was an exotic beauty, with a tinge of an accent.

Drew did the introductions and briefed the group that they were going to go through with the AK-47 buy that would, he hoped, nab them the Ghost.

"Frost has something he needs to brief us on." Drew filled Thad and Leila in on what had transpired that morning between Drew and Allie's assistant as they all settled around the conference table with cups of coffee.

"Allie's design assistant, Jason Kyoto, is Akira Kyoto and you're right Drew, he *was* yakuza."

With a remote, Frost turned on his computer and Jason's picture flashed up on a screen.

Damian Frost's musical Irish accent seemed wrong on such a dark man, as if the night had swallowed him whole and spat him back out. Allie sat close to Drew, keeping Damian Frost in her sight. She just felt better next to Drew.

"He's no longer in the yakuza?" Drew asked.

"No. He's out and he's being paid very well by Callie Carpenter."

Her sister's picture flashed up on the screen and Allie was surprised at her sister's appearance. She looked so different with short black hair.

"That we already know."

"Do you?" Frost asked, his gaze landing on Allie again.

Allie looked down to her hands. His eyes were so intent, as if the sheer power of them could burn her.

"Why are you afraid of me, lass? I won't hurt you."

Startled, she looked back up. Frost was staring at her and there was regret in his eyes. "I only eat little girls for lunch when I'm really hungry."

The fear and wariness drained out of her at his teasing. A kind tiger? Who would have guessed?

Frost drank from his cup and addressed Drew. "Like the Mafia, the yakuza in recent years have been forced to lower their standards when recruiting new members, and as a result some feel that they are neither as organized, nor as powerful as they once were. In the past, choice recruits came from the traditional *bakuto* and *tekiya*. That's the gambler and peddler classes, but today a rebel spirit and a willingness to commit crime for an *oyabun*, the head of the yakuza family, is all that is necessary to join the yakuza ranks. Most new members currently come from the *bosozuku*. In English, that means speed tribes, basically street punks known for their love of motorcycles."

"So, Kyoto was a *bosozuku?* What does that have to do with Callie?" Drew asked.

"Akira Kyoto was a street rat who had quite a reputation as a modern-day Robin Hood."

"He stole from the rich to give to the poor?" Thad asked.

"Aye, until he went into the yakuza," Damian replied.

"Why would a modern-day Robin Hood hook up with Sir John?" Leila asked.

"Exactly what I thought. Kyoto's interesting, but I think there's something you really need to know about Callie," Frost said, glancing at Allie. She felt her insides freeze up. Whatever he had to say, it wasn't good. She could see it in those intense eyes.

"If this concerns the mission, we all need to know," Drew said.

"It concerns the mission, Captain, since whatever happened between Kyoto, Callie and the yakuza stemmed from this particular deal."

"Tell us, Frost."

"Callie brokered a deal with Kyoto's *oyabun,* Fudo Miyagi."

A picture of a middle-aged Japanese man filled the screen. Allie thought he had mean eyes and didn't look as if he ever smiled.

"We are aware that she would broker many deals to seal her cover. It's routine," Drew explained.

"I agree, if this was routine. It's not. It was a huge shipment and Callie never collected a dime."

"So she gave up a shipment. Maybe it was a good-faith effort?" Allie said, her voice sounding defensive.

"I don't think so. Something went down the day the shipment changed hands. There were reports of gunfire and dead yakuza according to a police report. And, here's the rub—neither the shipment nor the incident were mentioned in Callie's field report. Right after that, Akira Kyoto severed his ties with the yakuza."

"She got him out. Usurped the *oyabun*'s authority." Leila said decisively.

"She wouldn't need to get Kyoto out," Thad said. "The yakuza is more like a club than an organization. A member can leave at any time. No, what Callie did for Kyoto was personal. I'd say if there's a threat against Callie's life, it stems from Fudo Miyagi. If he lost face that day—"

"He'd be out to restore it," Drew supplied the answer. "Kyoto mentioned Miyagi's name to me. Frost, look into Callie's hit-and-run in France and dig deeper. Find out what went down that day and how Kyoto plays a part in it. If there's a threat to Callie's life, I need to know who I'm dealing with and why. Allie needs that information to portray Gina Callahan."

"Aye, agreed. What about Kyoto? Do you want me to neutralize him?"

"No. Leave Kyoto to me."

Damian nodded. "You can count on me, Captain."

Allie said, "You don't seem surprised. You already suspected it was an attempt on her life, didn't you?"

"It's too much of a coincidence that a simple hit and run took down Callie. Something else is going on here. However, that's the least of our worries right now. The Ghost knows about the accident. His second in command contacted me this morning after you fell asleep. That's where I was. Frost."

A picture of a man flashed on the screen. He was handsome and well-built with a look that spoke volumes about hard living.

"What did he want?"

"He wanted to know if the rumors were true and Gina was dead. I told him that you were alive and kicking and ready and able to put the deal together. He wants to see you and insisted that you show up in a public place."

"Where?"

"There's a party at the British Consulate in four days. You're to be there and the Ghost will give you his terms for the shipment of military weapons we have for sale."

"I have four days to learn how to be Gina Callahan?"

"We can keep your contact to a minimum. It'll be quick and dirty and then we'll get out of there. I picked the consulate. The Brits will make sure to search everyone before they go in, so there'll be no weapons."

"Frost, bring up that file Mark sent you. Allie, pay close attention. We're going over Gina's acquaintances, friends, business associates, including her former boyfriend, Spike. You'll have time to study it later in more detail."

Once they went through the file, Drew said, "That's about it for today. I'll meet you all at the Watchdog training facility in thirty minutes. Don't be late. I also want you there tomorrow at 0600. Allie will need plenty of practice and an introduction to weapons."

WHEN THEY exited the building, Jason was standing on the sidewalk.

"I want to be a part of this, Miller. Callie would want me involved. One more layer of protection for Allie."

"She could use it," Drew admitted.

"C'mon, man."

"Follow us, but keep in mind, Kyoto, that I'm the team leader. What I say goes."

Jason gave a curt nod.

Thirty minutes later, Allie asked, "What is this place?" They pulled through a manned security gate located in an isolated area just on the outskirts of LA.

This used to be Camp Walker, named for General Walton H. Walker, who got the nickname Patton's Bulldog in the Second World War. It's a decommissioned fort that Watchdog has taken over. The main training complex has three dormitory buildings, a dining hall, a library, a classroom building, administrative offices, a large gymnasium and an obstacle course called Bulldog Run that is normally used by trainers to get new recruits into shape."

"Am I going to run an obstacle course?"

"No, Allie. We need to focus more on self-defense and get you up to speed on the world of spies and covert operatives."

"Thank you. I usually only run if someone's chasing me."

They pulled up to a squat white building with no markings and nothing to indicate it was a gym facility.

"It's so nondescript," Allie said.

"It's meant to be that way."

Pulling into a space, Drew and Allie exited the car and entered the facility.

She went into the women's locker room and took off her hoodie and sweatpants, revealing a T-shirt and shorts beneath. Shivering slightly, she grabbed a hand towel off a table by the door and exited the locker room.

Drew was waiting for her and he led her to a room with pads on the walls and floor. Thad and Leila were sparring and warming up. Jason was looking crestfallen, leaning against the wall and Frost was stretching.

Drew turned to her and indicated that she should fold

into a sitting position. "How much self-defense training do you have?"

"Not much. I took a course with LAPD about three years ago when I was in college."

"That's good. Let's face it. Five days of training isn't going to get you squat. What we can do here is to teach you some skills that'll give you live individuals to practice on, and make you more prepared to help yourself if you get into a hairy situation."

"I don't want to get into any hairy situations, Drew."

"I know, but it pays to be prepared. Self-defense is about using your brains, not your brawn. In fact, the tough part is your mind. Self-defense is about your body being yours and no one else's, about making your own choices and controlling your own life, and about doing whatever is necessary to stop other people from hurting you. Self-defense is not about hitting and kicking people."

"So I have to be some kind of Jedi Knight and use my mind to back them off?"

Thad chuckled and Frost looked at Allie, his dark, un-readable eyes hooded.

Allie shifted and said, "Sorry, I know this is serious. I really do, but it makes me crazy and I respond with jokes."

Drew leaned forward. "This is dead serious and you're not cut out for this, but we've got to make a bad situation work for us."

"Gee, thanks for the confidence, Obi-Wan," Allie said, deadpan.

Drew gave Allie a look that made her sit up straighter.

"Okay," she said. "I'm listening."

"What I'm going to teach you is simple. These tech-niques are for escape and evasion. There are other things you can do with them, but the main idea here is to give yourself some room to run, and some time to do it. Let's talk about strike points." He stood.

Allie followed suit.

"You already know where they are and what they do. You've known since grade school. If you poke someone in the eye, in the throat, hit them with a palm on the bridge of the nose, strike to the groin, kick them in the front or side of the knee—these will all hurt, distract, whatever—and it works on everyone. None of these points are covered by muscle, fat or any kind of padding. Size and condition doesn't matter. The only thing that matters is how hard you strike."

Thad moved in next to Drew wearing full body armor, with catcher's-mitt-like pads covering his hands.

"I'm going to demonstrate each move and I want you then to try it. Remember, strike as hard as you can. Thad is protected and won't feel a thing."

"Have a good go, sheila." Thad grinned.

"You want me to strike at his face?"

"I'll use the pads," Thad assured her. "No worries."

"To strike at the eyes and throat put your index and third finger together, curl the others to the palm."

He took her hand in his to show her the correct positioning. It was the first time he'd touched her since he'd kissed her in the conference room, and she was electrified by his touch.

She wanted him, and it had been so long, so very long since a man's touch had made her feel it to her core; a whole new level of thrill went through her. Her options were dwindling fast. Not that he wasn't a gentleman. He was, and no one had more control of himself than Drew—

just the thought of all that control was enough to make her want him even more.

He took a breath, letting her know that she wasn't the only one affected by this sexy thing between them, this hot, sizzling chemistry that worked like a drug.

"Don't hyperextend your fingers, merely hold them rigid. Strike straight forward into the eye or right above the hollow of the throat." He caressed her fingers into a spear-like configuration.

He demonstrated by jabbing toward Thad's face and Thad brought up the catcher's-mitt-like pad. Drew's strike went straight into the thick protective pad.

"For the throat jab, don't strike directly into the hollow, strike about one-half to three-quarters of an inch above it."

Drew put his full force into the strike and Thad used the pad to block. When he indicated she should do it, Allie moved into position and put all the energy she could muster into the strike.

When her fingers hit the pad, Drew nodded. "That's good, but don't pull your punch." He touched her shoulder and moved his hand down her arm, giving her goose bumps. "The force comes from putting your body into it, letting it flow from your shoulder down into your fingers. It'll only be effective if you disable someone. When he's down, you move out double-time."

She nodded.

"For striking at the bridge of the nose—"

"Can't that kill a person?"

"Yes, it can, Allie, but in our business it's kill or be killed. It's a good aggressive move, but if you have to use this move, you won't be on the offensive. Hit and run. That's what we're after here."

"It scares me, Drew," she said.

Leila snorted, Frost shook his head and Jason looked disapproving.

Thad gave her a sympathetic look.

"Captain, this is a mistake." Leila moved forward. "What was Murdoch thinking? She's a liability any way you look at it."

"He made the decision because Callie Carpenter is lying in a French hospital unable to fulfull her mission. We're very close to getting the Ghost. Allie's participation is a necessary evil."

"There you go again, being so positive," Allie said. She turned to Leila. "It's true that I've never done this before, but that doesn't mean I can't. I'm capable, but all this cloak-and-dagger stuff scares me. At least I'm honest."

Leila turned away in disgust. "And what's with scowling boy over there? What's in it for him?"

"My sister hired him to protect me," Allie answered, feeling the need to defend Jason even though she was still mad at him.

"You heard him. He wants to become part of the team," Drew said quietly, a warning in his voice.

Leila sauntered away from Drew and his warning. "A slot that has to be earned," she said.

Jason pushed off the wall. "You want a piece of me, *kifujin samurai?*"

"Lady Warrior. I like that. I want to see what you've got." Leila smirked.

"I got plenty, *kanojo.* But martial arts aren't about violence." Jason squared his shoulders and clenched his fists.

"We've got ourselves a Japanese monk." Leila scoffed.

He walked up to her and bent to look her in the eyes. "Believe me. I am no monk."

"No. You're a yakuza." Leila raised her chin, her gaze never wavering, a quiet challenge for Jason to defend himself.

Allie gasped.

Jason's lips tightened, but he said nothing. He pulled the black T-shirt over his head, revealing the extensive tattoo of a dragon he had on his body along with blue clouds, maple leaves and gorgeous cherry blossoms.

The colorful inked pattern covered him from collarbone to waist where the design disappeared into the loose-fitting black pants he wore. Allie wondered exactly how far down the tattoo went.

Leila studied the markings as she circled him. "Tattoos have always been an important part of the Hawaiian culture. Although I'm part Colombian, I recognize the meanings. Hawaiians embrace them as a form of celebration, a means of self-expression and membership in a tribe."

Jason moved his head to keep her in his sight. "Mine signals that I was part of a tribe, but not the one you think."

"Speed tribe?" she sneered. "Still a bunch of thugs."

Jason's eyes narrowed, but instead of getting tenser, he relaxed more.

"You shouldn't speak about things you don't understand."

Drew said very softly, "Leila, you would be the last person I would expect to throw stones."

She turned to him with a stricken expression. Her face flushed with shame and her eyes flashed with anger. Allie understood. It was Leila's shame that drove her to attack Jason. It reminded Leila of her own dishonor. Whatever that was.

"I would test him, Captain. It's my right as part of the

team just as it's part of Allie's training to learn self-defense. I know who I'm working with in her—a novice. But this man is untested."

Drew looked at Jason. "What do you say, kid?"

"I'm no kid. I lost that distinction a long time ago, Miller," Jason said.

"Your call, then."

"I will fight her, but I don't need to prove myself to anyone."

Allie wished she could be as sure and confident as Jason, faced with all these lethal people.

"What do you say, 893?" Leila taunted.

Allie whispered in Drew's ear, "Why did she call him that?"

"The yakuza are proud to be outcasts, and the word *yakuza* reflects the group's self-image as society's rejects. In regional dialect *ya* means eight, *ku* means nine, and *sa* means three, numbers that add up to twenty, which is a losing hand in the card game, *hana-fuda*. The word means *flower cards*. The yakuza are the 'bad hands of society,' a characterization they embrace in the same way that American bikers prominently tattoo the slogan Born to Lose on their biceps."

"Oh, so she's not being nice."

"No, she's not. Jason will have to hold his own."

"He's twice her size."

"Here's where you'll see that size and strength don't matter."

Leila attacked as soon as Jason bowed, but he was ready for her and flipped her onto her back with such a calm, controlled move, Allie was astonished and impressed.

Before he moved away, he sent his hand over Leila's shoulder and down her arm. "You have soft skin, *kanojo*."

Leila stood and laughed, not the reaction that Allie had expected. "Not bad, 893, not bad. You can stop calling me sweetheart. It's distracting while I kick your ass."

She came in low and, with one smooth move grabbed his fingers and had him down to the mat. He whirled his body, broke her hold and was easily on his feet, but not before his hand gently grabbed her ponytail, the strands of her dark hair filtering through his fingers. "Now we're even, *kifujin samurai,*" Jason said quietly.

The look Leila gave Jason was one of anger and… desire? Allie wasn't sure because Leila attacked again. They grappled, neither one giving any quarter, two hard, slick bodies battling for control. When Leila got the upper hand, she didn't hesitate. She brought him down. When she had him on the mat, she bent down and kissed him full on the mouth. "How was that, *koibito?*"

Leila was sweating. Allie had a feeling that it took a lot to make this woman sweat.

Jason looked so hot there on his back, his chest heaving from his exertions, the delineation of muscle and smooth skin covered in a sheen of sweat. He seemed lethal. His dark eyes held the secrets of the Orient, promises of both pleasure and pain. His hair spread out on the mat, gloriously black, streaked with red, wet at the tips.

Leila felt it. Allie could see it in her breathing and in her eyes as she stared down at him for a moment. He was an anime hero come to life.

"Lover?" he asked.

"In your dreams," Leila replied.

"I'd prefer anywhere, anytime, babe," he said, then Jason smiled, stunning Leila for a second, Allie was sure. Allie had been the victim of that man's smile when he was working for her. When she'd thought he was gay and she didn't have a chance with him. His smile could win any woman's heart.

With a move that only a pretzel could do, Jason rose and threw Leila off. When she came at him again, he manhandled her like a master, his hands all over her until Leila was swearing and growling like a beast.

Jason went in with a smooth move and threw Leila. Allie gasped as the woman flew toward her. Allie tried to move out of the way, but it was too late. Leila rammed into her, a stunning blow to the left side of Allie's body. Leila's momentum slammed Allie into the wall and they both dropped like stones.

6

THE VOICE came from somewhere on her right. She recognized it instantly—and it was definitely her sexy undercover watchdog. She quickly calculated the odds of spontaneously disappearing without a trace and figured they were pretty slim.

Too bad.

"Are you okay?"

"Yes," she whispered, and then confessed, "No." She didn't have the strength to maintain a lie. Leila Mendez had rung her bell but good. Her shoulder throbbed and the side of her temple stung.

"Do you want some water?"

Drew helped her sit up and all four members were standing around her. Allie was mortified that she'd been knocked unconscious.

"Hey, Allie," Jason hunkered down. "I'm sorry. I didn't mean for you to get hurt."

"Neither did I," Leila said, chagrined. "I'm really sorry. But, girl, you can take a hit. You weren't out for more than a few seconds."

Great. She'd impressed the warrior lady with her KO stats. "Thanks. I think." Allie wanted to stand, but was not sure she could.

She took the water Drew offered instead.

"Why don't you all hit the showers and get out of here? Allie and I'll meet you at the regular place."

They filed out and Drew helped her stand.

"Are you sure you're okay?"

"No, I've got the mother of all headaches."

Drew walked over to his bag and pulled out a bottle of painkillers. "I always need to take some after a session with that bunch."

A man with a plan that sounded like it could save her, which was his specialty, she guessed.

"They're tough and scary," Allie said, accepting the tablets from his open palm.

Her gaze rose to his mouth, and her blush grew even hotter. No one kissed like Drew Miller—long and slow, and wet and deep, like his next breath depended on her kiss, his mouth molding to hers as though they were made for each other, his body so strong and hard up against her, moving against her. She could have kissed him forever.

But things were getting complicated between them and she felt his withdrawal as keenly as she felt her headache deepen. "I'll just go get a shower." She limped out of the room with as much elegance and class as she could muster.

In the locker room, she sat down on a bench and tried to gather her composure. Jason was just as lethal as the others, maybe more so. He was a loose cannon, belonging to no one organization. She was thankful he was on her side. But a yakuza? Japan's most notorious organized crime syndicate? He'd been part of that? A thug? She wasn't sure she could ever trust him again.

What had her sister been thinking? .

That sobered Allie. Callie would not have hired someone

she neither trusted nor approved of, no matter what his skills were. Jason had somehow impressed her sister. Maybe when she was ready to forgive him for deceiving her, she'd ask him herself.

Allie thought about Callie lying in a hospital bed as a result of getting hit by a car that could have been driven by someone purposely trying to harm her sister. For some strange reason, all Allie could think about was the time when they'd run the three-legged race at a community festival. They had been way out in front, but Allie had tripped and fallen. Callie had forced her back up and they had ended up winning the race. Allie could never seem to follow through with anything, until she'd found design. Callie wouldn't want her to quit, not when it was so important.

Allie rubbed at her thigh, which throbbed in tandem with where she'd been hit in the temple. She stripped out of her clothes, grabbed a towel and headed to the showers.

Once under the spray, all her emotions washed over her, emotions she hadn't had an opportunity to absorb ever since this adventure started.

Her head turned toward a noise in the locker room. Had someone called her name? She turned off the water in the stall and opened the door to hear better.

"Allie?"

It was Drew's voice. Had she taken too long in the shower? The water had felt so good.

"I'm in here."

Drew walked in and her breath caught. It always did at the sight of him. He was wearing a deep red polo and a pair of tight, sexy jeans. His hair was damp and the five-o'clock stubble on his face only added a sense of danger to an already dangerous man.

Allie didn't even have time to reach for a towel. He was there in front of her, pulling her against him, taking her mouth like a man who had been denied sustenance for too long.

She shuddered, a delightful, eager sensation as he maneuvered her up against the stall and closed the door behind them. His hand delved between her legs and pressed against her clit and she cried out into the heat of his mouth. She sucked in a stunned breath and moaned when he roughly stroked over her breasts and her nipples hardened into aching points. He squeezed and kneaded her flesh and delicately pinched her nipples between his fingers.

She bit her lower lip to keep from crying out in pleasure. He kept her spine locked against the wall, and clamped his hot, wet mouth over one rigid nipple, sucking while his other hand came up to fondle her other breast.

Swallowing a whimper, she closed her eyes and gripped his waist. His velvet-soft tongue licked and swirled and his teeth nibbled, sending waves of heat rolling through her. Long questing fingers grazed her belly, and he took a step back to give himself more room to release the snap on his jeans.

"I need you to touch me, Allie."

"Take your shirt off, please."

He pulled the fabric over his head and her hands came up against his powerful pectoral muscles. She flattened her palms and simply ran her hands over the hard sleekness of him.

He pinned her again, his hard chest against the points of her aching nipples. His hands framed the sides of her face, holding her still as his mouth took hers, open and hot. His silky tongue thrust deep and tangled with hers, and he crushed his chest to her breasts, the heat of his flesh branding her. Widening his stance so that his knees bracketed hers, he rolled his hips, grinding his rock-hard sex against the notch between her thighs.

She moaned into his mouth and flattened her hands on the wall behind her. He jerked at his jeans and pushed them down off his hips until he had them off and away.

Then he was kneeling in front of her, his mouth open, hot and wet on her belly, his tongue stroking over her hip, his teeth nipping her mound. Her sex pulsed, ached and throbbed for the touch of his tongue, the caress of his fingers, the long, heated thrust of his cock filling her. He splayed his hands on her bare legs, widening them and bit the sensitive inner flesh of her thighs, making her gasp and tremble. The stubble on his cheeks abraded her soft skin, adding to her heightening need.

His palms slid upward, and he delved his thumbs between the slick folds of her sex, separating her for the taking. She waited, her breath suspended in her lungs as he leaned forward and buried his tongue deep. He licked and circled her sex, pressing hard, retreating slowly, teasing her to the brink of her climax, only to let her orgasm ebb.

Her hands clenched in tight fists in her attempt to resist the frantic impulse to grab the back of his head and increase the pressure of his mouth, the friction of his tongue.

"Drew," she said, and heard the desperation in her voice.

He looked up at her, his eyes dark and glittering with lust. "Tell me what you want, Allie."

She lost her breath, the words trapped in her throat. He went back to tormenting her further, laving her, suckling her, but keeping her release just out of reach. The pleasure grew with every hot pass of his tongue, heat and tension building higher and stronger. Her head rested against the wall and her body arched into his ravenous mouth, striving for the peak that was so, so close.

He withdrew, and she whimpered at the loss of contact. "Tell me," he ordered roughly, and licked her again. And again his tongue danced wickedly over her flesh, so skilled, warm and sleek.

Her frustration was so overwhelming, she sobbed and finally gave him what he demanded from her.

"Please," she panted, barely able to speak, but knew the one word would not gain her what she yearned for. "Please make me come."

A long, thick finger thrust inside her at the same time he closed his mouth over her clitoris and used the suctioning swirl of his tongue to draw her into a toe-curling, mind-bending, orgasm. A hoarse, ragged cry ripped from her throat as her climax crested and her entire body spasmed with the force of her release.

As soon as those internal ripples subsided and he stood, she went to her knees and took him directly into her mouth. He cried out and arched back at the suddenness of the pleasure. She moved her tongue around the broad, swollen head of his penis. His flesh was as hard as granite, textured like heated velvet and quivering with need.

She surrounded him with a silken caress of her tongue along the underside of his shaft.

She knew he was close to coming, she could taste the change in him, hot and salty, could feel the steady throb of the vein running along the underside of his cock, and his testicles were drawn up close to his body. A shudder rocked him, and she swirled her tongue over the engorged, sensitive tip, then closed her lips tightly over the crown and sucked, hard, pushing him higher, increasing his pleasure with each stroke of her mouth on his sex. He groaned, closed his eyes and pulled away from her.

His legs widened on either side of her as he lifted her up and onto his engorged cock.

She moaned straining toward him as much as her position would allow, eager to be filled by him.

He thrust into her and drove his hips up, the size and hot silken length of him stretching her as he impaled her to the hilt. She bit back a sharp cry, and he groaned and withdrew before plunging forward yet again, and again, moving against her.

He scraped his teeth along her shoulder, nipped at the side of her neck, and she whimpered as fiery, exquisite sensations spiraled down to her sex.

His face was taut with restraint, his unshaven jaw clenched, his expression a little savage. His hips pumped against hers, the muscles in his arms and down his back shifting and bunching beneath her roving hands each time he thrust deep.

A growl rolled up from his throat, and the length of him shuddered. He locked an arm around her waist, holding her still in ultimate control of her body, their movements and her pleasure.

He took her breast in his mouth and the skillful caress tore a low, ragged moan from her throat.

Her inner muscles clamped around him and she came in a long, shockingly intense orgasm.

He panted, sucking air into his lungs as he pushed into her higher, harder, deeper. Relentlessly. With a low primitive growl he finally surrendered to his own climax. He tossed back his head, thrust into her one last time, hard and fast, then stiffened. Her name tumbled reverently from his lips as his scalding release sent him over the sharp edge of pleasure and straight into the realm of mindless physical sensation.

Allie tried to calm her breathing as Drew slipped out of her.

"That's going to bruise," he said, his breathing just a tad ragged from having her up against the shower wall.

"What?" she replied, dumbfounded at the sensations that still moved through her, paralyzing her brain.

"Where you got hit."

She raised her hand to her face and felt her swollen cheekbone.

"I'm sorry," he looked so serious and grave.

She winced when her fingers touched a sensitive part of the bruise. "I should have been more careful."

"No, not about…I was talking about the sex. I was like a bulldozer."

"Oh, that." She smiled and wrapped her arms around his neck. "I like a man who knows what he wants."

"They should never have brought you into this."

He closed his eyes and turned his face away and her heart did a flip at the forlorn sound of his voice. She meant something to him, and she couldn't seem to help the thumpity-thump her heart made.

"But I chose to be in it. I'm in it up to my eyeballs."

"Beautiful eyes. Expressive eyes." He kissed the corners of her eyes, her cheekbones, careful with the sore one, the tip of her nose and her mouth.

"Flattery will get you everywhere," she murmured against his lips.

His pocket started ringing. Drew grabbed the jeans from the wet floor and pulled out his cell. "Miller."

He spoke into the phone, his dark, intense eyes flowing over her face and body like a river of fire.

He listened for a few seconds then covered the receiver. "Get some clothes on or there'll be a round two."

"And that's bad because?"

His face relaxed into a genuine smile and Allie melted. Round two sounded great to her. Just then her stomach rumbled. "Way to kill a mood, huh?"

"Makes my point exactly. We need to get out of here and get something to eat. We're meeting the team."

"I hope there's not going to be any more sparring. I don't think I can take it."

"Only verbal," he said.

He slapped her butt as she slid past him and she yelped.

"Watch out, Agent Miller," she said. "I know self-defense and I'm not afraid to use it."

"That's what I'm banking on, honey."

She walked away, sobering and sighing when her stomach rumbled again. A chill zipped across her wet skin as she grabbed up her towel. This was for real. She was going to face a very dangerous man tomorrow night. She was going to pretend to be a very dangerous woman with something very illegal to sell. Two of his teammates were skeptical about her abilities and one was overtly vocal about her misgivings. And then there was wild-card Jason. She had to wonder again what his stake was in it all. What had Callie done for him that had landed her sister in hot water? Someone wanted her sister dead.

And that someone could be hunting her tomorrow night.

7

THE SUN was just setting as they pulled up in front of Troppo.

"A dance bar?" Allie questioned. She didn't know what to expect from a bunch of undercover operatives, but a dance bar hadn't been it. She closed his car door and stood on the sidewalk, taking in the neon and the festive colors.

"Troppo's owner is a friend of Thad Michaels. They served in the same unit. Leila likes to dance." Drew shrugged. "It blows off steam for an upcoming mission. Leila can be wound tight sometimes."

"No kidding. She's got a thing for Jason."

"She'll cool down now that he's proven himself."

"No." She gave him a pointed look. *A thing.*

That gave Drew pause. "Naw. Not Leila."

Allie snorted. "Did you see the way she was looking at him when they were sparring and she kissed him?"

"No, I was watching Jason. He's a master."

"He was pretty impressive. I've never seen anyone move that fast."

"I have."

"Who?"

"Frost, but I think Jason might give him a run for his money."

"Your team sure is interesting. A big tough Aussie, who

is very much a marshmallow inside when it comes to women, a scary Irish dude who looks like an assassin, and a tightly wound jungle cat who, although small in stature, makes up for it with a tigress attitude."

Drew pulled open the door and Allie looked up at him, thinking how handsome he was. His hair just drying, the dark ends curling up. She reached out and touched them, sliding her hands through the damp warmth.

"They're all a bunch of international misfits, once on the wrong side of the law." He leaned his face against the palm of her hand. "Michaels was Australian Special Forces who worked the black market and after he got out, he somehow got involved with saving the President's life. I don't know the whole story on that one," he said when Allie opened her mouth to ask. "You'll have to ask him. He's worked freelance for the U.S. ever since. Frost's former IRA, but gave up that cause to fight for the U.S. for his own reasons. Mendez was Colombian-born, but she has a Hawaiian mother. Leila was a Colombian narco-guerilla and after helping the DEA, she went freelance."

"She's extremely beautiful. Have you and she, ever… you know?" Allie felt a surge of jealousy like acid through her veins.

"Never, she's a teammate. Unfortunately, I'm attracted to smart-mouthed, blond interior designers." Drew arched a brow and grinned sharply.

She punched him in the arm. "Unfortunately? Who's the smart mouth here?"

Large signs everywhere declared it was an open-mike night. A band was up on stage playing a very loud tune. People packed the place, but Allie saw Frost and Jason sitting at a table in the corner.

Allie and Drew made their way to the table. Jason and Frost both stood when she got there. Jason held the chair when she sat down. Somebody had taught them some manners in their misspent youths.

Leila and Thad came back to the table then and took seats, but Allie hardly noticed as Jason squatted near her chair and peered at her in the flashing light.

"You have a bruise on your face."

"Don't worry about it, Jason. It was an accident." She put her hand on his arm and smiled at him. It was time to forgive him. He so needed it.

He blinked a couple of times and gave her a tentative smile back, unable to hide the relief he felt. "Does this mean I'm forgiven?"

"Yes, you're forgiven and thank you for protecting me."

"I don't consider that done until you and Callie are both safe."

He meant it. She could tell by the tone of his voice and the unflinching steadiness of his gaze. The warmth of his caring settled inside her. "Callie will never be safe unless she gets out of the business she's in, Jason."

"I meant from the threat you both face. Fudo Miyagi."

"What do you know about that threat, Jason?" Drew asked.

"I wasn't sure before, but I am now. Miyagi is after Callie to regain face."

"What went down?"

"I met Callie as Gina, of course, when I was in the yakuza. She was doing a large transaction with him as a way to strengthen her cover. I had no idea she was a government agent."

"What did she do to humiliate Miyagi?" Drew asked.

"She ruined his reputation and rescued the woman he made his slave," Jason replied, his eyes lowering, his mouth tightening.

"Buying and selling women." Allie muttered, horrified that in this century such a thing was possible.

"It's big money in the East. A lot of girls and women are kidnapped from their families in the Philippines, China, Vietnam, Korea and Japan."

"Who's the woman?" Leila asked, her exotic eyes caressing Jason's face. His gaze was on the floor in front of him as he rose and sat down next to Allie. He just sat with his hands braced on the table, broad shoulders hunched, gaze fixed on a beer bottle in front of him. His expression was hard, closed and remote as if he had retreated to some dark place of solitude—or torment—within himself.

"She's my sister."

"That's why you joined the yakuza. To save your sister." Leila whispered as if only to herself.

"It was the only way I knew how. You have no idea how powerful they are. What they take they intend to keep, even if it's an eighteen-year-old girl. Even if it's against her will."

Everyone around the table was silent. Leila got up abruptly and walked away. On the dance floor, she grabbed a man and they began to dance. Jason watched her, that hungry look in his eyes that Allie had seen while they were sparring.

"What did Callie want in return?" Frost asked.

"Information about the organization's shipments. One in particular was a large shipment of handheld rocket-propelled grenades destined for Iraq. It was the real mission. She also made it a condition that I must leave the yakuza, which was easy for me to agree to as I only joined to rescue my sister. I didn't think that it effectively limited my access to Miyagi. Callie told me that I wouldn't want his blood on my hands. She was right. What he did to my sister was heinous and barbaric, but in the long run, there would have been no honor in taking his life."

"She's right, Jason," Frost said. "Revenge isn't a reason to kill someone. It gives you no peace."

"There's more," Drew said.

"Aye," Frost said. "Miyagi lost face, big-time."

Jason nodded and said, "Saving face means maintaining a good image, often in spite of adverse circumstances. The night we hit Miyagi was devastating to him. He lost the rocket launchers he promised to his client and these are people you do not cross. I can't imagine what he had to do to appease them. He lost his son's life by trusting Gina. Losing a son is a big deal in Japan because so much was invested in him. He was slated to take over the business. He also lost my sister—a woman who had the audacity to escape from him. The fact that Gina is a woman, as well, is even worse. His reputation was damaged, and in the gun-running world, his reputation is all he has. The only way he can regain face is to kill Gina. Everyone respects that in the world I live in. If he doesn't kill her, he's done."

"And you?" Frost asked. "What part did you play?"

"She made me stay out of it so that I couldn't be blamed. She brought me my sister and made arrangements for her to come to the U.S. and disappear. That's when she told me her real name and that she worked for Watchdog. She knew what the score was and that Miyagi would probably come after her. She hired me to protect Allie." Jason rubbed the back of his neck. His eyes were full of the gratitude he had for Callie Carpenter and the bravery and compassion she'd shown to him.

"So you haven't seen your sister in all this time?" Thad asked in a low voice.

"No. It's to protect her. If Miyagi knows where she is, he'll try to get her back."

Allie took in a quick, hard breath.

Thad raised his beer bottle. "To Callie."

Everyone replied and clinked their bottles. "To Callie."

"Hey, pass the fries, Wizard," Frost said.

"Wizard? Why did you call him that?"

"That's his nickname. He's the Wizard of Oz. We all have them. It's a military/operative thing," he said, stuffing a fry in his mouth.

"What is Drew's?"

"Captain America."

"That's why you call him Captain."

"Yeah."

"And yours?"

"Dublin." Frost shrugged.

"What about Leila?"

"Five-O," Leila said as she sat down, her face flushed from dancing.

"I want a nickname, too."

"How about Tinkerbelle?" Drew suggested.

"That doesn't sound dangerous."

"I don't know," Frost said, "she seemed like a vicious little pixie to me. She sure didn't like Wendy and had no qualms about selling her out to the lost boys."

"You know *Peter Pan?*"

"The author was a Scottish bloke, wasn't he? My ma read it to me in Ireland when I was a wee lad."

"Oh, I see." Allie said, warming up to the name. "I like it. Wait, what about Jason? He needs one, too."

"No, I don't," Jason said, leaning back in his chair.

"Kid Kamikaze," Leila said, looking at him for the first time since he'd told his story.

Jason rolled his eyes.

After about an hour of watching people dance, Allie felt herself begin to fade, even if it wasn't late. Drew threw down money and took her by the arm. "Time to go, Tinkerbelle, or is it Sleeping Beauty?"

She didn't protest, just smiled sweetly at him.

At the loft doors, he kissed her. "You know Prince Charming woke Sleeping Beauty with a kiss." Allie smiled.

"Are you awake?" Drew asked wickedly.

"Hi-ho, hi-ho, it's off to bed we go?"

He laughed as he pulled her into the loft.

FOR THE NEXT two days, Allie was drilled by all the team members until she fell into bed at night thoroughly exhausted. She would have to make time to talk to Drew about Lily's house. She must finish that project and do it soon.

When Drew roused her on the third day of her training, she groaned with the muscle aches and the bruises on her body. "Please, no more."

"Allie, no more physical training, I promise, but we've got more to teach you—how to communicate back to the team safely, how to use the transmitting device that will go in your ear, mission codes and procedures. Oh, by the way, Frost called. He was able to trace the car—the one that hit your sister."

"This is all so surreal."

"Mark called and said that your sister is doing much

better. She wanted to talk to you, but it's not a good idea to agitate her at this point."

"When can I see her?"

"In a day or two, once you've completed the mission. It's best to minimize your contact for now."

Allie nodded, happy that her sister was improving. She wished she could speak to her but knew she didn't want her sister to worry. Allie rose and got dressed.

When she sat down at the breakfast bar, Drew put down a plate of waffles in front of her. Allie forked up a bite and chewed, and then said, "I don't think I can stuff any more information into my head. What's next?"

"You're going to learn the difference between role-playing and acting."

"There's a difference?"

"Yes. One will get you in. The other will get you killed."

"Then it's really important to outline which one I should be doing."

"Role-play. Undercover work is not at all like acting," he said. "Undercover officers are taught to role-play. The difference is that while actors can take time to learn their lines, undercover officers have to immerse themselves in a role and be able to respond to constantly changing circumstances.

"Anything that you say or do can compromise your safety, the other people working with you, as well as jeopardize the mission. Actors get a chance to stop, rehearse their lines and call time-out and reshoot if they make a mistake. We don't get that option. We get dead."

"Drew, I'd rather go back to kissing you. That was a whole lot more fun."

"Uh." He ran his hands through his hair and gave her

a don't-go-there look. "I was trying to not think about that, Allie."

"Maybe you'd better start calling me Gina. Does that help?"

"No. It doesn't help, but it's a good idea."

"So who is this crazy chick my sister portrays?"

"She doesn't *portray* her, Allie. She *is* her."

"Okay. Who is she? What does she like to wear?"

"Check out the garment bag and the suitcase Frost dropped off the other day. That's her stuff."

Allie went over to the suitcase and opened it. Clothing fell out. Well, scraps of clothing anyway. There were tiny mini skirts in leather and denim, skimpy mesh shirts and tight, tight jeans. Her hands shook as she picked up a black garment and some pink tulle and held them up.

She turned to Drew. "A bustier and a tutu? What is this girl? A cross between a dominatrix and a ballerina?"

Drew's eyes were riveted to the bustier and he didn't speak for a moment.

"You're imagining me in it, aren't you?"

"Hard not to."

"Let's focus on the role-playing part and then we'll practice."

For the majority of the day, Allie listened diligently to Drew and they practiced. Finally, as night fell, Drew held up the garments and told Allie, "Time to look and be the part."

Allie grabbed the clothes and headed for the bathroom, but stopped dead and turned around when Drew spoke.

"She's been known to go without underwear under her miniskirts," he said with a gleam in his eye and a smile on his face, but Allie turned the tables on him.

"Commando? Oh, damn." She turned and headed for the bathroom. "It's a good thing I've done all those squats at the gym. If I have to moon anyone, at least my ass will look good."

Drew groaned as the bathroom door closed.

He swore silently, praying that he would keep a cool head. It wasn't his head that was hot right now. It seemed his dick had a mind of its own. Being plastered up close and personal to Allie couldn't possibly be smart. Damn karma when you needed it. It could go from good to bad in sixty seconds.

She was a contradiction of sweet and tough. When he'd thought for sure she'd cave, she hadn't. When he'd thought she'd respond one way, she'd respond another. In his line of work, unpredictability was something that he had to deal with every day. But Allie tied him up in knots and made him think that it would be really fun and interesting to get her to release all those knots, one by one.

There he was going down harder than a bad guy at the end of his scope. Only this hurt a whole hell of a lot worse.

He didn't do relationships. He'd made that clear. Hadn't he? He wasn't one to make promises he couldn't keep. Like in Afghanistan. He'd made promises to the men who'd served under him. Many of them hadn't gotten out alive. Too close. He'd gotten too close to his platoon. That's when he'd gotten out, gotten drunk for days, then he'd made sure he worked alone. His team really didn't count. They could all take care of themselves, all as well-trained, as tough as he. He'd picked them just for those attributes. If one fell in battle, it would be due to his or her own carelessness and not his judgment.

His father always told him to move on. Never let his

emotions get in the way, don't make ties. It had worked to his advantage when he'd gone into the military and followed in his father's footsteps. After all, what was a military brat supposed to do when the life he knew was so fragmented? The military and military training all felt so…familiar.

The sound of the door opening at the far end of the loft brought his head up. She was coming out of the bathroom. Or so he thought. Nothing else happened for the next few seconds, except he slowly rose to his feet from where he'd been sitting.

He was sure of what he'd expected, but when she finally walked through the door, he knew he'd just been outclassed, outgunned and stripped back to private. All he could do was stand there and remember to keep his jaw off the floor.

This was it. This was what he had been worried about since he'd first met her. His heart did a double-flip and he felt as if his brain had just melted.

Dressed to kill. Now that was a metaphor that described her to a T. Her hair was pulled on top of her head in a haphazard ponytail, her glorious mouth was painted a deep, dark red and way too much of her silky skin was exposed. Way too much.

And the outfit. So help him, he couldn't stop wondering if she had gone commando under the pink tulle. All it would take was a flip of that flippy skirt to find out. The road to hell was paved with good intentions. This was one of his best intentions. The black bustier fit her like a second skin, molded to her torso. Allie's muscle definition was awesome. Not overworked, just sleek and cool-looking.

His eyes went back to that froth of skirt pulled down to

the point where it crossed the top of her legs. She'd chosen a pair of thigh-high boots, leaving a swath of silky skin between the tulle and the leather.

With the dark sunglasses covering her expressive eyes, she was bad-ass. Gina "Bad Ass" Callahan. She looked like sex and hot fudge over cherry ice cream—melt-in-your-mouth delicious.

All he had to do was keep from getting caught in her bad-ass trap himself.

Right. That's all he had to do.

He did not have to let his gaze slip and slide around her curves. He didn't have to stand there, sending up silent prayers of gratitude to the gods of leather, or wondering what had happened to the laws of physics—he felt as though he was floating, as if she'd sucked all the gravity out of the room.

She kept walking and he found himself backing up until his spine was so flat against the wall, it was as if a 250-pound bruiser had pushed him there with sheer strength, not this slight, 120-pound beauty who had transformed herself in less than half an hour.

She placed one hand on his chest, and with the index finger of her other hand, she pulled down the shades just enough to peek over them. Her cool eyes studied him like a bug beneath a microscope.

"Is this what you had in mind?"

Even her voice was stronger, more defiant, like Tinker-belle with an edge.

All he could think was that he wanted all her pixie dust on him.

"Ah, yeah. You know I was kidding about the com-mando part, right?" he asked, wanting the words to come out as nonchalant, but in his amazement, his voice cracked. He cleared his throat.

"Were you, really?" She smiled, looking as satisfied as a dominatrix snapping her whip, knowing that her victim has just surrendered.

She tilted her head, the movement sliding all that gorgeous blond hair to her bare shoulder where it slipped and slid around. The movement made her look more Allie and less Gina which should have alleviated some of this heat he was feeling deep in his gut and groin, but it only intensified the dichotomy between sweet and tough.

"I would believe your tough macho detachment if it weren't for the fact that your heart is beating really hard, Drew. Ka-thump, ka-thump, ka-thump. Thrumming like a live wire."

"Speaking of live wires, let's channel all this energy into the task at hand, Allie...ah Gina, and get you to think like her, as well as dress like her."

Allie's bottom lip came out in a pout. "You're starting to be such a drag, Mr. Federal Agent. A big, draggety drag."

"It's about keeping us all alive, honey. And if that makes me a drag, then bring it on."

With that she backed up.

"It's time to take the show on the road." He grabbed her hand and pulled her toward the door.

"Where are we going?"

"To Hell and Gone."

"What? That whole lake-of-fire, burn-in-eternity thing doesn't really work for me, and I really don't like to sweat."

"It's time to learn how to be bad-ass."

"Oh, no. I think I'm going to be sick."

8

Abandon every hope, ye who enter here.

ALLIE READ the plaque on the door as they stood in front of one of the roughest, toughest bars in LA—Hell and Gone.

"You brought me to a dive bar? Are you nuts? They'll eat me for lunch and pick their teeth with my bones."

"Not as long as I'm here. I just want you to get the attitude, Allie. It's just observation," Drew told her.

"Sure," she said, giving him a glance that told him he was twice the idiot she thought he was if he believed that.

"We'll just get a drink, play a little pool and leave. If you want to assert some of that attitude, go ahead. I'll cover you."

"Great, you've got my back, but who'll cover yours?"

"I've got all the cover I need."

"I know that's not alpha-male crap because I've seen you in action. It's just a statement of fact."

"I want your body language to say "don't mess with me." Watching other people who already have that attitude, helps. It's a lesson pure and simple. You don't need to become a new person—you just need to be comfortable with yourself and your flaws. By being comfortable with yourself, you show that you don't care what they think of you."

"I don't care what people think of me."

"Yes, you do, Allie, and it shows. Lose it."

"Easy for you to say," she said under her breath, but Drew heard her.

Hell and Gone was living up to its name as Drew and Allie entered. A wall of heat and steam came pouring over the threshold. Drew put his hand on the small of her back and pushed her forward. The temperature inside the room had to be close to a hundred degrees.

"The first ring of hell," Allie said, eyeing all the people. "Are you sure we have to do this? School never looked like this."

Hell and Gone was packed to the rafters with a boisterous crowd of misfits, outlaws, hipsters and goth wannabes.

He and Allie moved deeper into the place, skirting the dance floor where people gyrated to the very loud music on the stage.

Allie took a barstool close to the edge of the bar and Drew settled in next to her. "Shabby chic takes on a whole new meaning in here," she said, her voice filled with sarcasm.

The bartender came over and Drew ordered a beer. Allie surprised him by ordering a shot of tequila. She crossed her gorgeous legs, garnering her plenty of stares. The men in the club were all focused on her, their eyes taking in every curve. Drew felt proprietary when he knew he had no right to feel that way. He wanted to break their faces, but instead he tried not to radiate any kind of protective quality over her.

"You're not going to believe this," she whispered. "But there's a switchblade in this skirt's pocket. A switchblade in a Tinkerbelle skirt."

"Leave it in there. It's illegal to carry a concealed weapon in LA."

"You're carrying a gun."

"I have federal ID and a permit."

"Oh. Right."

She watched the people in the room and after her third shot, Drew shook his head at the bartender when he started to move toward her.

She swiveled on the stool and eyed him. "Who do you think you are? If I want to drink, I'll drink," she said belligerently.

"Allie," he whispered.

"Let me try this out," she whispered back.

"It's Gina. Gina Callahan. You've forgotten already?" With that she ordered a fourth shot and picked it up, moving toward the patio and outside. Not liking that one bit, Drew followed her.

It was then that he got separated from her.

A bouncer put his hand on her arm and said, "You can't drink on the patio."

"Really? What kind of lame rule is that? This is a bar after all, and I'll drink where I want."

Other people started shouting that she was right and surged forward until the bouncer was pushed out of the way and a flood of people emptied onto the patio. Drew got jostled and pushed with the others and for a moment he lost sight of Allie.

Then he spotted the damn Tinkerbelle skirt. Jesus, she was going to be the death of him. He started shoving through the crowd, pissing off plenty of people, but he didn't care. His chest felt tight and his stomach seized. He never panicked. Never. But Allie was making him lose his cool and fast.

If anything happened to her…

Then he heard it and his blood ran cold.

"Gina!"

Of all the places in LA he had to bring her to, he'd chosen the one club where she might be recognized. He got close enough to see Allie whirl. At least she was responding to the name. She faced the man who'd called out, and double damn—it was Gina's old boyfriend Spike.

Richard Van Dorn aka Spike had only recently been in prison. Exactly where Callie masquerading as Gina had put him for gunrunning and loan-sharking. He was pretty sure that Spike didn't know it had been Callie who had played him and put him behind bars.

Allie recognized him from the photo Drew had shown her that morning. She seemed to freeze, then surprisingly she loosened up. Spike took her by the arm and started to drag her away from the others. They were heading for the back alley that ran the length of the street. Drew doubled his efforts to get to her, but by the time he got to the mouth of the alley, they were nowhere in sight.

AT FIRST Allie let the guy drag her, but then remembered that Gina Callahan wouldn't allow anyone to drag her anywhere. She dug in her heels and snapped her arm out of his grasp.

"What do you want?" she asked, some of the anger in her voice real.

"To talk to you. I haven't been able to find you since I got out. It's too noisy back there."

"I don't want to talk, Spike. It was fun, but now it's over. I have other things to attend to."

"I like the blond hair. When did you decide to go Valley Girl?"

"Right after the police busted you. I felt the need to look different, less like Spike's girlfriend."

She turned to head back up the alley and back to Drew when Spike grabbed her arm again.

"Actually, Gina, what I really want to talk about is the hundred thou you owe me."

Allie frantically tried to recall the whole incident that had to do with Gina and Spike and when it came to her, she felt utter relief.

"I lost a lot of my own money that day, and the guns. The Feds took it all. I was lucky to get away. I had to run, Spike. I hate to run. You know that. I think we both have to cut our losses."

"I heard you're doing pretty well. Thought the rumors of you cut down in France were true—finally, the hand of death caught up to you. But here you are, whole and healthy. I think you still owe me." He pressed her against the dirty wall and Allie gasped as his wiry body slammed into her.

Self-preservation had her reaching for the knife in the skirt's pocket and with a desperate flip of her wrist it opened with a whirling sound. She pressed it into his stomach and said very succinctly. "I have…a…a knife."

She sounded too hesitant and weak, so she tried again. "It would be a terrible shame to have to gut you, Spike. Let me go. Now!"

He laughed, which wasn't exactly the effect she was going for.

"I love it when you play rough, Gina."

His head descended, and Allie decided kissing him was not an option, so she did the only thing she could think of, because gutting him was obviously not an option, either.

Allie was sure she wouldn't be able to handle all the blood involved with such an act.

She brought up her knee and it connected solidly with his groin. He was writhing on the ground as Drew came running out, almost colliding with Allie in the dark.

While they stood there, she flicked her wrist again and turned her back on Spike. "Breaking up is hard to do, Spike. Consider this your break-up call."

"You owe me, bitch!"

In the two seconds before Allie answered, she did something amazing, something Drew wouldn't have thought any raw recruit could have done in such a short time. It was all so subtle that if he hadn't been fixated on her, trying to get a clue as to how freaked she was right now, he would have missed the actual transformation. As it was, he saw the whole thing take place in the space of a single breath.

Turning to face Spike, she put herself between Drew and Spike in an I'm-in-charge stance—so subtle, so smooth and so damned unexpected.

"I don't freaking owe you anything. Cut your losses, Spike, or I'll cut them for you." Her tone was pure menace.

"Gina!"

"Screw you."

He couldn't have scripted it better. She inclined her head to Drew and they both walked away, leaving Spike cursing and holding his nuts as if they were shattered into a million pieces.

As soon as they were out of sight of Spike, Allie folded like a table after a reception. Just simply dropped. Drew caught her against him and cradled her like something rare and precious.

ALL THE WAY back to his loft, he kept glancing at her as she slept in his front seat. Still amazed by her performance, he couldn't seem to take his eyes off her.

He stopped the car at the curb in front of his loft and just sat in the seat and stared at her. She reminded him of how she had looked in the bathroom at the government building. A heartbreaker in the very true sense of the word. Damn good at getting herself into jams and getting herself out of them just as easily without his help, mind you.

She looked like hell, sleepily drunk with mascara tracks down her cheeks and her deep red lipstick making her lips look all the more red, all the more kissable.

"It's not polite to stare," she said.

"I'm not that polite," he responded.

"No, you're not."

Swinging around to the passenger side, he reached for the door handle, then stopped. He needed to remind himself—again—that he was here to train her and nothing else.

He opened the door and simply stared. She was doing something so amazingly simple. Stretching, but it became something more when a woman in a too-short skirt arched her back and lifted her hands over her head, yawned and pressed one of her two-inch boot heels into the floorboards.

He called it arousing. Mesmerizing. She was nothing but silken, golden tan all the way up to her…he averted his eyes with effort, getting angry all over again that she'd gone out in public without underwear. He didn't dare think that the tattoo—whatever it was—was bare to anyone who happened to flick up the edge of that skirt.

"Come on, ball-buster. Let's go," he said, but actually getting her out of the car proved to be another of the night's long list of challenges. The tequila had turned her body into a Slinky, and the harder he tried to hold on to her, the slinkier she got.

"Hell," he muttered, finally just bending his knees and lifting her over his shoulder. He clamped his arm across her thighs, locked his car and headed for the loft elevator.

"Man, I was scared," she said, her voice kind of raw and throaty.

He heard a distinct sob. It was the aftereffects of fear. He knew clinically that it was extremely natural, but he didn't like to hear her voice go all watery. Crying wasn't one of the things in his operative manual. He'd rather go one on one with a guy with a very sharp knife.

"Things got out of control, but you handled it."

"I did. Like a pro with a switchblade in her fluffy, girlie skirt. I'm sure I looked real tough." Her words were slurred and Drew figured that the tequila was kicking in.

He set her down because he was sure she'd flash whoever happened to be out and about. Once she gained her feet, he held her against the elevator wall as it began its smooth glide up to his apartment.

Suddenly, the lights went out and the elevator ground to a halt. Power outage. Damn fine timing. He was trapped in the elevator with a crying woman.

She let out a squeak and rammed into him so hard it knocked the breath out of him. The emergency lights came on in the elevator and bathed her upturned face in a dim, warm light.

With her makeup messed up, her face had lost some of its dramatic contrast, but none of its beauty. Her lashes weren't so dark. Her lips were now a softer shade of pink. He could see a light dusting of freckles across her nose, which made her look younger—a lot younger than she had a right to look. Her hair was wild, absolutely wild, as if she'd been dragged across the pillows, and was he…crazy, or lucky or simply out of his ever-loving mind?

The tracks of her tears took hold of his heart and just wouldn't let go.

"Yeah, especially telling Spike to eff off."

She opened her eyes all the way and laughed. "Yeah, that's me. Tough girl."

"Have you ever said *fuck?*"

"No. As a matter of fact I haven't said that word and I don't intend to. It's vulgar."

"Interesting. You won't say the word, but you'll go commando in public."

"I'm not naked. I have on a thong. I couldn't quite bring myself to go all the way."

It was his turn to close his eyes and let that information wash through him. She might as well be naked beneath that skirt. A thong, for Pete's sake.

"Allie, you're killing me by inches."

"I'm dying, too. Every time you look at me with those intense, secret-agent eyes. What hides in them I wonder? How did you get here?"

"One step at a time, Allie."

She smoothed her hand over his face. "You're so beautiful, so amazing. All I want to do is touch you. All the time."

"That's not a good idea."

"You keep saying that. Drew." She breathed his name, her hands going to the buttons on his shirt and starting to undo them one by one.

"I'm not fragile and I'm not fickle. I understand what it takes—what kind of character it takes to protect your country. My brother, Max, is a warrior through and through. You have the same look. He thinks that to protect people, you have to keep everyone at arm's length. It just isn't true. It only isolates you from the very people you're trying to protect. I think you lose something. Something important."

He didn't stop her. Neither her words, nor her hands. He was too busy thinking, remembering and wondering if she might have learned some black magic in that bar. He felt a little bewitched, as if he were under some kind of spell. He also remembered the taste of her mouth, and her in his arms, and yeah, that was probably enough to get him into deep trouble—quicksand trouble.

"It's not that easy, Allie. It's never that easy."

She was pulling the rest of his T-shirt out of his pants and unbuttoning his cuffs, pushing his dress shirt off his shoulders. She was gone, over the edge, hopped up on adrenaline and tequila. Part of him wanted to go over the edge with her. She was scared, hungry and she needed him.

Needed him inside her.

Needed him to anchor her world.

And that was something that he couldn't do. He couldn't anchor anyone's world because he was always on the move. He had to remain rootless. Hell, even the loft belonged to Watchdog. He owned nothing and liked it that way.

Relationships were like possessions, they got in the way. He'd learned his lesson the hard way in Afghanistan, the hardest way, and he knew better than to kiss her.

He moved his hand up to cup her cheek and smooth his fingers over her skin.

Hell, they wouldn't still be together after this mission

anyway. She'd go back to her safe life and he'd continue to do what he did best. Move on.

Yeah, he knew better than to kiss her, but he did it anyway—just let go of every freaking thing he'd believed in forever, tilted her face toward his and brought his mouth down to hers.

Heat, as pure and simple as anything he'd planned, washed through him. He groaned with the pleasure of it, gave himself over to it. Her skin was damp, and he was breaking out in a sweat, and he suddenly knew that nothing mattered. She wanted him, and deep inside where he'd locked away his own emotions, his own needs and desires, he wanted her, too.

One of her hands slid through his hair, across the nape of his neck, cupping his skull, keeping him captive for her kiss. He reached for her leg and drew it up around his waist, pushing up her skirt, getting her closer, reveling in the silken softness of her thigh beneath his fingers. Her other hand was siding under his waistband, going downtown, driving him wild, and the anticipation of her taking him in her hand and stroking him made him groan.

The elevator lights came on and Allie sighed. Drew swore and the elevator door opened with them standing there with her hand down his pants.

"Let's go, Captain," she said. Pulling her hand out of his pants, she grabbed a handful of his shirtfront and pulled him out of the elevator toward his loft door.

"Key," she demanded, holding out her palm.

He pulled his keys out of his pocket and found the right one.

"Come on," she said, doing that gimme motion with her fingers.

He gave her the key and, without letting go of him, she

opened the door. He'd never been manhandled by a woman in his life, never been given orders or followed them, but Allie was magnificent in her need for him, and he couldn't deny her the pleasure of anything, including his body.

With the door open, she pulled him inside, dropped the keys on the floor and bumped the door shut with her hip.

"No phones," she searched for his cell and found it in his front pocket, way too close to his engorged cock. But that wasn't her focus…yet. His whole body went hot just thinking about that.

She flipped open the phone, pressed the off switch and flung it onto the couch. Way out of his reach. Even if he wanted to dial 911 in this particular emergency, he couldn't. Not that he wanted to.

"No clandestine meetings, no training and no excuses."

She turned the lock on the door and threw the dead bolt.

"No interruptions."

"Allie—"

"No," she said, interpreting the tone in his voice all wrong. He was just going to suggest that she sit down. She was shaking and holding on to him as if her life depended on it.

"I have never had such a hard time getting what I want, Drew. Now, maybe if Jason hadn't been gay…wait a second, that's right. He's not gay. It doesn't matter anymore. I should have seen it. He's so much like you."

"In what way?"

"Cute, but with that edge all women love. We love the danger. Who doesn't dream about getting hot and heavy with James Bond, or, in Jason's case, Vincent Valentine?"

"I don't."

She ignored his comment.

"Who's Vincent Valentine?"

"Final Fantasy." She reached out, and the muscles of his stomach flexed as her cool, slender fingers caressed the heated skin of his belly.

Final fantasy? There was nothing final about the way her hand traveled up his body but there was his every fantasy about her fingertips grazing his tingling skin. Nothing final about the way she encircled his nipple, leaning forward and putting her slick, wet tongue against the tip.

His head dropped back. She swirled her soft tongue around his hard nipple, grazed the length with her teeth, and nibbled the tip before taking him deep into her mouth and sucking hard.

His breath hissed out between his teeth, and he slid his hands into the silk of her hair, kneading her scalp.

Moving to the other nipple, she nipped him again, making him twist in the agony of the pleasure she was giving him with her sweet mouth and teeth.

She flattened her hand in the center of his chest and skimmed her cool palm downward, her fingers dragging over his ribs and taut abdomen. She didn't stop there, and he gave a raw moan of pleasure as her fingers curled along the thick length of his erection confined behind denim.

His body jerked in response when she stroked him, and it was all he could do not to rip her clothes off and take her right there, on the floor.

She wrapped her arms around his neck and brought his mouth down to hers to finish the kiss she'd started in the elevator. The pressure of her mouth parted his lips and her tongue slipped inside to tangle with his. Her fingers threaded through the hair at the nape of his neck, her leather-clad breasts crushed against his chest, and the car-

nal mating of their mouths generated enough heat to make
them both spontaneously combust.

He slid his hand down her side and over her hip. Bunching
the tulle in his hand, he methodically raised it until his hand
encountered her bare thigh. His hands cupped her firm bottom and she thrust her hips forward in an uncontrollable
movement that set them slightly off balance. Catching the
waistband of the thong with his crooked thumbs, he pulled
it down her legs far enough for her to toe it off. Cupping her
creamy thigh, he lifted her leg, dragging it over his hip and
brought the core of her heat right against his groin.

She gasped against his mouth as he thrust against her,
the sweet friction making him crazy for her bare, slick skin
against him.

He used his back muscles to springboard off the wall
and start to move toward the bed, releasing Allie's thigh.
She did a one-eighty and pushed him toward the bed until
the mattress hit the creases of his knees.

Her hands went to the waistband of his jeans. Desire
darkened her eyes as she pulled at the button and lowered
the zipper.

"Tight fit," she said, her voice husky and soft.

Taking both denim and brief material in her hands, she
pushed it off his hips. "Oh, man. Man, oh, man, you're
beautiful," she breathed. "So beautiful."

He leaned forward, touching his mouth to her temple,
kissing the soft skin. His breath ruffled the wisps of hair
along the side of her face, and pure, undisguised sexual
energy crackled between them, a rare and irresistible
chemistry that intensified with each moment that passed.

Her body responded, automatically readying itself for
his possession. No words were spoken—none were

needed—as she lifted a hand and curled her fingers around the nape of his neck. She pulled his lips to hers and kissed him deeply, avidly. His mouth was equally hot and eager, his tongue bold. And greedy, consuming her with rich, un-adulterated pleasure.

They pulled back just long enough for him to quickly strip off her bustier. Their mouths met again, lips open, teeth nipping and nibbling, tongues touching, tangling. Her hands swept over the broad expanse of his chest, and she plied his nipples with her thumbs, and then strummed her fingers downward to his taut belly. With a groan, he smoothed his hands along her shoulders and filled his hands with her breasts, rolling her nipples back and forth between his fingertips.

He felt out of control, and he embraced the untamed sensation along with the freedom to do things with and to this woman that he'd never explored with another lover before.

He felt as if she were a piece of him he'd never known he'd been missing. When he'd first laid eyes on her, think-ing she was Callie, the connection had been that sudden, that intense.

Her hand found him and his entire body jerked as she closed her fingers around his cock. He slanted his mouth across hers again with a rough growl, his tongue thrusting deep as he reached beneath the miniskirt she wore. Skim-ming his fingers up her thighs, delving into the crease between her legs, he found that she was already wet, al-ready excruciatingly aroused, drunk on passion and the ex-citement of the forbidden. He found her clit with his thumb and strummed across the knot of nerves in a sleek caress. All it took was that one electrifying touch and she came in a fast, feverish climax that left her panting and gasping for breath.

Breathing hard and aching for her, he moved backward, falling to the bed and bringing her with him.

He reached over to the bedside table and grabbed up a condom, sheathed himself and then he was tugging her toward him, forcing her legs wide-open on either side of his thighs. Grasping her waist, he guided her to sit astride his hips, and his cock slid along her slick flesh and unerringly found the entrance to her body.

He pulled her hips down at the same time he bucked upward, sinking into her tight heat and embedding himself to the hilt. She inhaled sharply at the abrupt invasion, and he groaned long and low. He rocked her pelvis against him, his body tense and quivering. She grabbed on to his shoulders, easily picked up the rhythm he set, and rode him with utter abandon.

The material of her skirt floated around them, covering where they joined, which added to the eroticism of their union. His hand roamed up her spine, and his fingers fluttered along the nape of her neck, then wrapped the strands of her hair in his fist. He pulled her head back with that one hand and used the other to splay against the middle of her back, forcing her body to arch into him and her breasts to rub against his chest.

Their bodies were locked tightly together, and she continued to ride him as he scattered soft, damp, biting kisses along her throat and over the plump slopes of her breasts. He circled his tongue around one rigid nipple, blew a hot stream of breath across the peak, and then did the same to the other. He lapped at her slowly, licked the taut tips teasingly and nibbled until the madness was too much to bear.

Grabbing a handful of hair at the back of his head, she pressed his parted lips to one crest in silent demand and he obeyed, taking as much of her breast as he could inside the wet warmth of his mouth.

He sucked, and a whimper of need slipped from her lips. He felt the convulsions that started deep inside where he filled her, full and throbbing. She moved on him harder, faster, and came undone as a torrent of exquisite sensation flooded his limbs and sent him careening into an intense and fiery orgasm.

He released a harsh groan of surrender, then gripped her hips, rocking her in time to each frantic upward surge of his thick shaft within her. She wrapped her arms around him, holding him close, and his body shuddered in and around hers in long, deep, powerful spasms.

When it was over, they stilled, their arms and legs entwined, both of them too wiped out to move. Chest to chest, the wild beating of their hearts was all Drew could feel in that seemingly endless stretch of time, that profound connection between them was all that mattered.

9

"THAT WAS a new one," Drew said, panting.

"What? Having a woman force herself on you?"

"You're like an all-out commando team bent on destruction."

"Lock and load," she said softly, a small smile turning up the corners of her mouth.

He nodded, totally turned around now. She simply up-ended him. He propped himself on his elbow. Looking down into her eyes, he smoothed his hand up the side of her face and ran his fingers into her hair. It was hard to imagine that she hadn't felt something of what had hit him so hard.

She shifted beneath him. It was a small movement, but enough to send a bolt of pleasure shooting straight through his body. He was in no-man's-land right here. Right now. A place he'd never been before because he'd never let himself slow down long enough to find it.

But the night cocooned them and seemed to close out the terror and bad guys bent on making the world a much uglier and unsafe place.

It was staring him in the face, exactly what she'd said to him. She was the reason he put his life on the line again and again. Only a handful of people knew what a toll it took on the men and women who actually sacrificed everything day in and day out to help give them their idyllic lives.

Allie was tangible; thinking of her as just some person didn't apply anymore because he knew her. He'd touched her, had her open up to him about her fears. He'd seen her courage in the face of fear.

He kissed her, lowered his mouth to hers and simply indulged himself. She touched him with her tongue, tasting him, and he returned the favor, letting himself just get high on her kisses, her mouth so wet and warm and lush. Easing onto his side, he pulled her close and slid his hand down her back, molding her to him.

He couldn't go back to his detachment. He couldn't shake the feelings hitting him from all sides like mortar fire.

Skimming the skirt down her legs and off her body, he dropped the pink tulle onto the floor.

"What exactly do you have tattooed on your backside?"

"Oh, you saw that?"

"No, just a glimpse."

"I'll show you." She flipped over and Drew finally got a view of the tattoo. It was a broken heart with the word *Heartbreaker* beneath it.

"Is this a warning?"

"No, silly. I got it when I was sixteen. If my parents ever found out, I would have been in so much trouble."

"Why did you get it?"

"There were times when I loved being a twin and times when I didn't."

"The tattoo made you different from your sister?"

"Yes, but only I knew it. It gave me my own identity," Allie said, her gaze caressing his face. "You, on the other hand, don't have any tattoos, but I want to look anyway," she murmured. Her hands were all over him. His mouth was all over her. Every place he kissed her, she tasted like a promise kept. Every place she touched him, she left a trail of fire.

When he'd taken all he could, he sheathed himself with another prophylactic before settling over her. Leaning down, he kissed her cheek.

He entered her in careful degrees, kissing her the whole while, being careful not to put too much of his weight on her, or too much of himself inside her too soon.

It was an all-out tease that tested his very resolve.

She moved against him, lifting her hips ever so slightly. He pulled almost all the way out of her, before slowly sliding back in. She arched her head back with a soft purr, and he ran his tongue down the length of her throat. She was so beautiful. Her breasts plump, her nipples an electrifying coral. He leaned down and captured one with his mouth and sucked, so gently. She groaned, and the sound went straight to his balls, making them tight. This was heaven.

She was so responsive, so languorous and so incredibly hot. She was melting for him, and she was so wet. She was also incredibly beautiful—her nose so delicate and refined, her cheeks so soft and her mouth…

Yes. Her mouth.

He slanted his lips over hers and thrust into her again. He wanted her to come. He wanted to feel it. He wanted to know she'd come for him again—and he wanted to give her pleasure, mind-blowing pleasure, because he wanted her to stay.

To stay with him for days and weeks and months, maybe forever. She rocked his world hard, and he wanted to know everything about her.

Carefully pulling all the way out, he moved down her body, kissing her softly on her belly, following the contours down to the silky insides of her thighs. His heart was racing.

Slipping his fingers through her curls, he opened her for his kiss. She caught her breath with a shocked gasp, and then released it in a soft whimper when he licked her, his tongue gliding over the sweet center of her arousal again and again and again. She stiffened, and he felt a rush of pleasure so intense he groaned. His hand tightened convulsively on her waist, holding her still for his delicate assault.

She cried his name and opened her legs for him even wider, surrendering to his mouth, to his fingers sliding in and out of her so very, very gently. He wanted to push her right to the edge and take her down the other side in a long fall. He wanted it to be exquisitely good for her, more pleasure than she could ever have given herself. He wanted to give her a guaranteed, soul-shattering orgasm she would never, ever forget, not if she lived to be a hundred.

Caressing her, he slid his hand up her torso and down her arm, taking her hand in his and bringing it to his mouth. He sucked on her fingers, then moved back up her body to suck on her lips. He kissed her over and over again, loving being with her, being on top of her and feeling her getting more and more turned on.

Cradling her head with one hand, he took hold of himself with his other and checked to make sure his condom was still in place before he fitted himself back inside her. He pushed in slightly and held himself still.

"Damn, damn," she murmured repeatedly, a soft sound deep in his mouth, her hips lifting toward his, and he pressed himself deeper, dying just a little, but not going all the way, not yet. The torture was too sweet. He wanted to play with her and tease her for as long as was humanly possible, with no rules save one. He wanted her to come, hard, urgently, all over him.

He lifted himself above her, resting on his forearms, and moved himself in and out of her in a lazy, heat-inducing rhythm. She was small, so slight and yet so female. He gave her all of himself. She took all of him with a groan of longing.

"Drew." His name was barely a breath, uttered with such need he leaned down and kissed her cheeks, her brow. He was here, with her. He wouldn't leave her, not ever. Her leg came around his waist, holding him more closely to her as he pumped, and she groaned his name again.

Damn. He felt it, too, the edge of pleasure turning sharp and soulful.

"Drew." She tossed her head, her hands grabbing him on either side of his waist, pulling him deeper, holding him tighter.

He hesitated, and then thrust, making her wait for a heartbeat or two in varied intervals, slipping his hand between them to stimulate her. It didn't take much before her body went taut beneath him, his name sighing from her lips, urgent and wanton.

"Drew…don't…please, yes."

He was in such a haze. He understood her perfectly, his mouth wet on hers, her body balanced on the edge. He slid his other hand up the length of her arm, twining his fingers through hers, rocking into her again and again until she came, her breath catching, her body pushing up against his, holding him deep. She gasped his name, and he went rigid, releasing wave after wave of the purest ecstasy. It rolled through him, making it hard to breathe, impossible to think.

At the end, he felt transported, his body in some sort of limbo. He rested his forehead on hers, but other than finding his breath, didn't even try to come down. He was so high. His muscles were twitching with latent pleasure, his mind floating in the ozone of total physical and mental relaxation—and he would have stayed there for as long as he could have possibly ridden it out if he hadn't bent down to kiss her and tasted her tears.

"Allie?" He rolled to his side and wiped her cheek with his thumb. He knew he hadn't hurt her. She'd been with him, right there with him, every single second. "What's wrong?"

"Nothing. Oh, Drew." She sighed, kissing his face, his mouth, her hands sliding over his chest.

Yeah, he thought, understanding dawning on him. He was just lucky he wasn't crying, too. He'd never felt anything like what had just happened between the two of them. Never. She was hot and sweet and soft and smart and funny and tender and wild and brave.

He kissed the top of her head as she snuggled up against him, relaxing into sleep, the movement of her hand slowing into a lazy caress.

He was a fool to believe that idyllic life was for him. He'd been in the dark for what seemed like forever. It was where he lived and thrived. And he did it alone.

He had to do it alone.

THE SOUND was sharp and loud in the night as Allie came awake with a snap and sat straight up in bed. Drew was rigid next to her. She turned on the light over the headboard. She looked at Drew as he twisted in his sleep, bathed in sweat, thrashing as though he was in pain.

"Get to cover! Get to cover, Martinez! Don't worry about me! That's a fucking order!"

She felt completely out of her league, which wasn't anything new. She'd never had to deal with a man who'd been through what Drew had been through. She froze when he yelled again.

"No. Martinez. No."

She put her hand on his shoulder and shook him.

He exploded into action. Lethal muscles trained to kill flipped her off the bed onto the floor. He pinned her there, his eyes glazed with pain and something so dark and terrifying Allie felt sheer terror pierce her heart.

"Drew. It's a nightmare. You're having a nightmare," she shouted into his face. And he jerked at the sound of her voice, his eyes blinking rapidly.

He took a shuddering breath. She could feel him trembling as he looked down into her face. "Allie, damn." He looked so disoriented, so vulnerable that her heart sank in her chest. He moved off her and reached down to help her up.

She put her hand in his and rose slowly.

"Are you hurt? Did I hurt you?"

He was still trembling. She went to put her arms around him and he sidestepped the move almost too casually as if he hadn't really meant to. He sat down on the edge of the bed.

Allie stood there for a moment then answered. "No. I'm just startled. That's all."

"Good. Good," he said, looking down at his hands as if he expected to see something there. He seemed transfixed, and she moved forward, unable to watch him do something to himself even if she wasn't sure what it was.

She placed her hands over his palms, and he jerked and looked up at her.

"What?" she asked, searching his face.

He shook his head. "It's nothing. I'm just wired."

This time when she wrapped her arms around him, he didn't move, so she held him, not moving herself, feeling some awful premonition in the rigidity of his body, as if he might crumble if she so much as dared to breathe.

She didn't know what to do for him, how to help him.

He pulled away and she felt the distance he put between them. It scared the hell out of her. She'd been a total fool to get involved with him, to let her heart get even a bit tangled—and it was tangled, without a doubt. He was going to break it into a thousand pieces and she wasn't sure if she had the strength to survive that.

He'd been right in all his warnings, because right now his withdrawal hurt pretty badly.

Here today, gone tomorrow.

Tomorrow hadn't even had time to come and he was already gone.

"We should get some sleep," he said. "We've got a 5:00 a.m. wake-up call."

She nodded and returned to her side of the bed. She could feel his gaze on her, lingering on her body, her face, her hair. It was agonizing to know that he wanted her, but on limited terms. Sex okay, intimacy not okay.

She had no one to blame but herself.

She got into the bed, expecting him to turn his back and remain aloof.

She gasped softly when he slipped his arm around her

and pulled her close to his body, spooning her against the
seductive heat of him. For the second time that night, tears
collected in her eyes and tracked down her cheeks.

The ugliness of what he must have endured didn't re-
pulse her. Witnessing his fears and pain only made it harder
knowing what kind of man held her. An American hero,
torn up inside over a nightmare she was sure had at one
time been real. Very real.

His agony only firmed her resolve to do what she must
do, be whomever she must be to get this job done.

THE POUNDING on the door woke them both and Allie
scrambled for the sheet that Drew flung away from him to
get to the door. He stopped, realizing that he was in his al-
together, and headed back to the dresser and managed to
slip on a pair of sweats.

But it was too late. Wood splintered and three bodies
came through the door, weapons drawn.

"What the hell!" Drew shouted.

All three had been crouched and ready for a fight, but
when they saw Drew half-naked and Allie completely
naked except for the sheet, knowing looks blossomed in
three sets of eyes.

"It's seven, sir. We thought something happened to
you."

"Cell phone?"

"We've been trying to call you since 0615, sir."

"Damn, that's right. It's turned off."

Allie was still breathing hard, adrenaline running
through her system. To make matters worse, Jason walked
through the door.

"Allie, are you okay?"

"Thad, fix the door. Frost and Jason, go get breakfast, and, Leila, make the coffee."

With his orders, they all hopped to it. Except Jason, who lingered as if Allie needed his help.

"I'm fine," she said to him, touched by his concern. She wrapped the sheet around her body and got out of the bed. So many eyes followed her to the bathroom she felt that she was being scrutinized. When the door closed, she took a deep breath and leaned against it. Great. Now they all knew she'd slept with Drew.

"Don't take too long. You need to eat before we go," Drew called from the other side of the door. He was right, of course. She needed some sustenance. But she couldn't get last night in the elevator out of her mind. She remembered how warm his skin was, and how much she was fascinated by his mouth, the hard, broad strokes of his muscles. She'd been thinking about tracing every line of muscle with her fingertips…and her tongue, and then suddenly they'd been kissing, his mouth so hot on hers. That memory was worth remembering, but now everyone out there knew that they'd been naked together. How did she get herself into these situations?

"Allie?" His voice came again, a little more insistent.

She needed to pull herself together and get going instead of standing in the bathroom completely losing it.

"Could you go away…please?" she said through the door. Like to Siberia for a few days, so she could slink away like the coward she was and hope never, ever to have to face them again.

After a long silence, during which she began to wonder if he actually had gone away, he spoke.

"No, I can't go away." He didn't sound any more pleased

about it than her, which made her feel even more mortified. "We've got a lot of work to do today, and it all includes you. If we can get some food and water in you, you'll feel better."

She'd get through this. She always got through horrendously embarrassing moments.

It was only one more thing to handle. After what she'd gone through with him, and the nightmare, she could feel the distance. Although she wanted intimacy from Drew, she had to accept that he might never give of himself. Now, she felt as if he'd walled himself off completely from her.

More training. She sighed. After a quick shower, she rummaged around in the suitcase to find something appropriate. She found a pair of tight black shorts that would work well along with a small white T-shirt and a black hoodie. She pulled her hair into a ponytail and secured it with an elastic. She washed her face and brushed her teeth. Grabbing up the hoodie and a pair of sweatpants to ward off the early-morning chill, she exited the bathroom.

Thad had already jury-rigged the door and everyone else was drinking coffee and eating croissants, except Drew, who was standing near the bank of windows, separate and alone.

His team knew something was different; they kept giving him glances. Drew was off his stride and everyone knew it and they blamed her. She could tell this when his team members looked at her.

"Coffee?" Jason asked.

Allie took the cup, poured in cream and took a sip. It was delicious. "Thanks, Jason."

He nodded. "Allie, can we talk about what you're doing?"

"I've already given my word. I've quit too many times in my life, Jason. I'm following through on it."

"But Callie would be totally against this. She hired me to keep you safe. She wouldn't want you to put yourself in danger, not for this."

"That's because she doesn't think I can handle it, Jason. My whole family thinks I'm a ditz, who doesn't think before taking action. Even you think it."

"Allie—"

"I don't want to talk about it. You've shown where your loyalty is and it isn't with me. Callie's paycheck I'm sure is much more than I could pay you."

"It's not about money."

"All I know is that I can't let Drew down after all the time and effort he's put into this. I'm the only one who can do this."

She turned away from him and the protest on his lips. She could hear Thad giving him encouragement and sympathy. Her eyes met Drew's. For a moment the world drifted away and she remembered every sensation he'd given her last night from the touches and sex to holding her against him as if his life depended on it. For an unguarded moment his eyes were full of emotions she couldn't name.

He looked away from her. "Let's move out, people."

10

THE SETTING SUN glistened off the pool, liquid spilling from a rimless waterfall. He tipped the crystal glass to his mouth and tossed back the twelve-year-old Scotch.

Unable to enjoy the view from his opulent office, he paced the length of the huge floor-to-ceiling windows, his tie loosened. Even amid the lushness of the vineyards and tranquil, rarefied atmosphere up here on his hilltop, he felt unsettled, unsatisfied and very close to losing his focus. A focus he'd had for five long years. He reached out and opened the latch to the window, breathing in the pine-scented air. His eyes were blind to the panorama city-scape below.

Gina.

Only hours separated them. At the consulate party tonight he had every intention of making sure he had one-on-one time with her even if he had to take out her body-guards and lackeys. In person, he'd pressed her second in command, but he wouldn't budge. Her life was threatened and no one would get personal time with Gina.

There had to be a public meeting place and the man had been smart enough to suggest the consulate party. There would be no weapons allowed on the grounds with so many dignitaries attending.

It guaranteed that the only people who would be carrying weapons would be consulate security.

He'd done plenty of digging and found out that Fudo Miyagi was the one who'd tried to mow Gina down in France. After finding out that Miyagi was desperately searching for handheld rocket-propelled grenades, Jammer contacted Miyagi and set up a meeting. He had every intention of neutralizing any threat to Gina.

A relationship wasn't in the plan. But for better or worse, he'd connected with the woman the first time they'd met. He'd kept his real emotions hidden from her, not because he couldn't trust her, but because he couldn't trust himself.

He ached for her, felt his chest grow tight remembering the last time he'd seen her. Had it been only just over two weeks?

She'd gone limp, draped over him like an exhausted kitten, her mouth partly open, her lipstick gone, her mascara smudged beneath her eyes—the whole of her so lovely it broke his heart. Five feet six inches of golden curves and a tiny tan line across her ass.

The Chinese food they'd ordered had cooled considerably. He checked the wontons, counted only three, and put them back on the side table. He went instead for the shrimp dumplings, stretching the chopsticks over to the far side of the table and snagged the wire handle on the container.

He'd just put one in his mouth when he felt her stir again, as if this time she might be waking up.

Chewing slowly, he watched and waited, practically holding his breath—just one more act of pure idiocy he was at a loss to explain. He always kept breathing, always, even under fire. He breathed.

But, oh, no, not with her. She was a threat of unknown capabilities, unknown force.

What if he loved her? What then?

She yawned and, yeah, that's about all it took for him to start getting real interested in her waking up, and with both of them naked and her right next to him, there was no way to hide it.

He was starting to feel uncomfortably vulnerable, something he would have thought it would have taken a guy pointing an AK-47 at him to accomplish—not one beautiful woman whose only weapon was a one-way ticket to heaven.

Before she even opened her eyes, a slow smile curved her lips.

"Hey, don't bogart the food or I'll have to get rough with you."

"Mmm. Sounds like fun. Open your mouth."

She obeyed—which gave him a really nice feeling—and, using the chopsticks, he placed a dumpling on her tongue. She sighed in pleasure.

Oh, yeah. Open your mouth, Gina. *Lick me.*

He wondered what she was thinking right then.

He didn't have to wait long to find out.

Without so much as a subliminal suggestion on his part, she started sliding down his body, one of her hands going between his legs and the other sliding up his chest, under his arm, and over his biceps. There her fingers curled around him—as if she needed to hold him down to keep him from getting away.

Yeah. Right. Just the thought of having her mouth on him had been enough to make his erection complete, and given her position, there was no way for her not to know it. Perfect. Again.

Her tongue came out and lit him on fire. He braced one arm against the headboard and gripped the sheets with the other, his hips rising off the bed on a surge of pleasure so intense if he'd been standing it would have put him to his knees.

Oh, man, be careful what you wish for. His gaze was riveted to the utterly compelling sight of her going down on him—her hand encircling him, her mouth all tantalizing softness and flickering movement. Her hand slid over his belly, tickling the dark hair arrowing down his lower abdomen, and, as he watched, she ran her tongue up the length of him.

Good grief. His hips rose again, and he gripped the bed harder. She was relentless in her tender onslaught, and he was very quickly floating somewhere near to where nirvana must be, his body suffused with pleasure, moving in rhythm with her, his thought processes on permanent vacation.

"Gina," he said, his voice hoarse, his body strung out on the rack of her mouth. "Gina…"

She had to know what was going to happen; try as he might, he'd hit an unmistakable rhythm—and it felt so incredibly good, so sweet and deep.

"Gina…"

Her only answer had been to slide her hand across his shoulder and up to his face. She gently traced his lips, silently telling him to *shh,* and he caught her fingers with his mouth.

She had to love him. He felt loved—loved in every cell of his body.

He kept pulling her up, until she had to release him and give him her mouth. He wanted her kiss like nothing else in the world. He wanted to be covered by her.

She was a part of him. They were both sheened with

sweat, their bodies so hot he felt as if they were fusing into each other, a sensation that only increased when she slid down on him, taking him inside.

With Gina on top, her hot pelvis sliding against him, he brought her face down to his and just lost himself in kissing her, in thrusting into her, in letting her ride him.

When she tightened above him, her cry caught in her throat. He still didn't stop. He kept going, pumping into her, holding her mouth to his for an endlessly deep kiss. Eventually, his release overtook him and dragged him completely under, with her.

He was a damn fool.

Everything he'd done so far had been planned, methodical. For one purpose only. Now he felt fractured, his focus splintered. He should have sent someone else to deal with Gina Callahan. If he'd only known what kind of deep kimchi he would end up in.

He hadn't been this screwed up since Colombia where he and so many had died.

Yeah, the day he'd died and become the Ghost.

As a ghost he had no life except for the one that his oath had wrought. He'd play out the hand he had. He'd intended to follow through no matter the sacrifice.

But it had been so long since he'd wanted a woman.

Now he just wasn't sure if he could sacrifice everything, especially Gina.

"YOU EXPECT me to wear this…this swatch?"

"It's what Gina would wear, Allie. It's part of the character."

Allie threw the material and it snaked down Drew's body until it pooled on the floor at his feet.

"No way am I wearing that in public. It barely covers me."

"Allie, be reasonable. It's part of the disguise."

"Usually a disguise *covers* body parts, not reveals them."

"You have to wear the dress, Allie."

"Fine," she said, grabbing the fabric from the floor. But before she could get away, he captured her around the waist. "Do you think I want you displayed for everyone to see? Do you think I like the fact that you're walking into danger?" He looked down into her blue eyes. "Hell, no. I hate it. But we have no choice. The Ghost has to go down. Do you understand?"

She trembled in his arms and he pulled her closer, the last two days wearing on them both. He felt as if he was losing her increment by increment, until she would disappear like smoke and he'd find himself alone again. Alone and isolated, just the way he liked it.

Yeah, that's right. The way it had to be. When this was over, could he walk away and go on to the next mission?

He felt raw inside. He needed her, wanted the feel of her in his arms because she was real and he loved her. How stupid, how cruel that he should fall for a woman who made him want to stay. He couldn't tell her because he knew it couldn't last.

"Do you understand, Allie?" he asked again in a hoarse whisper.

She nodded against his chest and his broad shoulders rose and fell. He turned to pace, but her small hand settled on his arm, holding him in place as effectively as an anchor. He studied her angel's face and the air fisted in his lungs. She gazed at him with sparkling blue eyes that mirrored the need that ached in his soul.

"Yes, I understand. I understand, Drew."

He closed his eyes against a wave of pain, leaned down and brushed his lips against her cheek.

She took his hand and led him to the bed. With a yank, she pulled his towel off.

They made love, immersing themselves in the desire, steeping themselves in the experience, savoring the tenderness. Gentle touches. Soft, deep kisses. Caresses as sensuous as silk. A joining of two bodies and two souls, one scarred and one as bright as the sun. Straining to reach together for a kind of ecstasy that would banish shadows. A brilliant golden burst of pleasure. Trying desperately to hold on as it slipped away like stardust through their fingers.

And when it was over and they rose to dress, Drew stared out into the dusk that fell and wished with all his heart that he didn't have to let her go.

INSIDE the consulate, her hand gripping the stair rail, she stood in a crowd of people above the main foyer. There had to be a hundred guests here.

Her hands shook and she tried to still them. Gina Callahan wouldn't shake. Gina was going into one of the biggest deals of her life and she would have her war-face on. Allie reached for her own inner courage and quelled the shaking. She took a deep breath.

Callie would have been so proud of her. Allie's throat ached suddenly thinking of her sister. She prayed she would get a chance to tell Callie all about her incredible adventure.

"Are you okay?" Drew asked in her ear.

She nodded and together they turned and walked into the grand ballroom. More people milled about her. With a nonchalance she hoped didn't look fake, she grabbed two glasses of champagne off a tray as a waiter walked by.

Sipping, she looked around the room.

"Do you see Jammer?"

"Not yet, but when I do, you'll be the first to know."

She nodded, feeling better when she saw Leila stroll by on Frost's arm, both of them breathtaking in their evening wear. Women followed Frost with their eyes and men did the same to Leila.

Jason was in the back of the room at the bar and Thad was walking around with a tray of champagne.

She was covered on all sides.

When the soft music started, Allie needed to find a restroom. She turned to tell Drew, but some woman in a blue sequined dress had a death grip on his arm and was talking to him avidly. Figuring it wouldn't take long, she headed toward the bathroom.

HE WATCHED her move away from her second in command and it was all the time and space he needed. As soon as she came out of the restroom, he snagged her arm and pulled her into a hallway, then into a vacant office.

"Gina."

She gasped softly and it was more than he could take. He pulled her close, felt her soften against him, felt her hand slide up to his shoulder, and for the first time in days, the knot of tension that had been holding his heart in a vise began to ease. It was dangerous, letting go of the tension, but for her he was willing to do it, on the chance he could draw some of her inside himself, some of her heat, some of the life pulsing through her.

Gathering her closer, he bent his head to hers and eased

her backward in a slow dance of swaying hips and barely moving feet. If it had been up to him, he wouldn't have moved at all, just held her and run his hands over her, buried his face into the curve of her neck, remembering.

"Gina," he murmured. "I thought you were dead."

He wanted to forget who he was for a while, and she was the one, the only one who gave him that kind of oblivion.

"You changed your hair. I like it." His mouth came down on hers. Go slow, he told himself, even as he slid her dress up over her hips, a very short trip, especially when she stopped him with her hand on his.

Fine. He just wanted to touch her. He'd just wanted to breathe without it hurting in his chest, but kissing her was working. He let another barrier fall away, opened himself up more, just to take her in, just to get closer to her heat.

Wrapping his hands around her waist, he lifted her onto the desk and moved between her legs, getting there, closer to where he needed to be. Everything about her turned him on, which was such a relief. Everything had gotten so messed up.

Everything.

So damned messed up.

He pulled her against him, fighting off a tiny surge of panic. Something wasn't right.

Another surge of panic sizzled into his veins, and he held her tighter, kissed her harder—too hard. He could tell by the weak sound of distress she made deep in her throat. She pushed against him, and for a second, just a second he wondered if he was going to let her go. He was locked onto her like a heat-seeking missile, and, so help him, all he wanted was more. He didn't want to back off, and it crossed his mind that if he just kept at it, it would feel right.

But it didn't.

He broke the kiss and stared down into her eyes and he knew.

He grabbed her by the throat and asked, "Who the hell are you?"

IT ONLY TOOK a few moments to notice that Allie was gone. The second Drew couldn't find her he headed for the restroom where he'd seen her last.

He spoke into his mike. "Anyone seen Allie? I've lost her."

"No, Captain, there are just too many folks," Thad said. "I'll start looking."

"Miyagi's people are here," Jason said quietly into his mike. "I recognize some of them."

"Tread carefully. They might recognize you," Leila offered.

"I'm going to look for Allie," Drew said. He went into the alcove where the restrooms were and walked inside calling out. "Gina?"

No answer. Damn, where was she?

ALLIE COULDN'T BREATHE with the hand on her throat and effectively couldn't answer the man. She clawed at his hand, saw his handsome face contort.

"Where is she?"

Allie managed, "I can't breathe. Let go." All her self-defense training flew out of her head as the air dwindled. He let up, but effectively cut off her escape route.

"Who are you? Where is she?"

Allie had no time to think, she just blurted out. "I'm her sister. Her twin, Tina."

The man's eyes narrowed, taking in her features. "Are you joking? Where is Gina?"

"She's been hurt and I had to take over the sale. We don't want anyone to know she's incapacitated." Allie held on to her composure. "I understand this isn't a normal transaction with my sister in the hospital, but if you still want to deal…"

"I do," he growled. "I need the weapons and I don't particularly care where they come from. But you should have been up front with me from the beginning. I don't like surprises."

Allie nodded. "Then we have a deal."

"On one condition."

"What's that?"

"Who put your sister in the hospital?"

"Why do you want to know?"

"Give me the information or we're done," he hissed.

"Fudo Miyagi," Allie replied, looking up into the cold steel of his eyes.

"So, it is true. It was Miyagi."

"We traced the car back to one of his people. He wants her dead because—"

"I know why he wants her dead. Where is she?"

"In the hospital."

His smile was brief and without any amusement. "Don't play games with me, lady."

"How can I trust you? She's my sister."

"I won't hurt her. She's…one of kind. Give me the information. Now."

"Trust goes both ways, Jammer."

"I don't trust anyone. If something doesn't seem right to me, I'll kill you. That's a promise, so don't screw with me. What hospital?"

"Pitie-Salpetriere."

"If you're lying to me—"

"I'm not. Where and when do we meet to exchange the guns?"

"Tomorrow night at nine at the Port of Los Angeles, Berth 271."

Allie's head dropped, so her chin touched her chest. She took a breath and nodded. When she looked up, he was gone.

Slipping off the desk, she straightened her dress and pulled open the door. As she stepped into the hall, she smelled smoke. Someone in the main ballroom yelled, "Fire!"

Allie turned to look for smoke and screamed when she saw an Asian man pointing a gun at her.

Before she could draw breath to scream again, Thad came out of nowhere and ran at the man, who got off a shot. She saw Thad jerk and grunt, but the Asian man went down under Thad's weight.

As if in a dream, time became strangely elastic, stretching, slowing, but Allie's perceptions became almost painfully sharp. The white walls of the hall hurt her eyes, the smell of a gun's discharge was acid in her nostrils, the sound of the bullet leaving the chamber shrieked in her ears.

11

SHE TURNED to run and hit solid muscle. A man grabbed her by the hair and pulled her back so he could look into her face. He had a knife and he pressed it to her throat. "Mr. Miyagi wants to talk to you."

Allie didn't want to talk to Mr. Miyagi, ever. Somewhere between her normal life and the intense self-defense classes she'd found her instinct for survival. She brought up the palm of her hand and hit the man as hard as she could on the bridge of the nose. He staggered back, yelling.

Surreal, she thought dimly. This couldn't be happening. She couldn't be yelling or lashing out at this strange man. This couldn't be the real world, because everything in her field of vision had instantly become magnified, as if she were shrinking and shrinking.

"Gina!"

It was Drew's voice and she turned toward him, just as something sliced her thigh. Allie went down as Drew came barreling along the hall at a full-out run. Jason right behind him. Four more men were coming in the opposite direction, all Asian, all looking at her with purpose in their eyes.

She got up and started to run. Drew and Jason passed her, yelling, "Get out, Gina!"

Drew and Jason were outnumbered, but soon Frost and Leila dashed past her and engaged. It was an all-out fist-fight, but Allie couldn't watch. Snatching up the thick linen napkin Thad had had draped over his arm while he'd been serving, she ran to his side and knelt down.

She turned him over and cried out. "Oh God, Thad."

Pressing the napkin to his wounded shoulder, she held it tight.

"No worries, sheila," he said, his voice weak.

"Don't die. Please don't die."

"Take more than a bullet to kill me." He patted her hand.

"Don't you dare say it's just a flesh wound," she warned.

He laughed then winced in pain. Allie could hear sirens in the distance. She looked back. Of the four Asian men, one was down and the others were fleeing. Drew and his team let them go. He ran back to Allie as the consulate security came racing down the hall.

Allie kept up on the pressure on Thad's shoulder, even with the blood oozing through the cloth and staining her hands.

At last the ambulance arrived and the E.M.T.s took over. Allie insisted on going with Thad, and at the last minute, Frost pushed himself inside the ambulance door. The E.M.T.s tried to protest, but Frost gave them one of those chilling looks and they shut up.

The last she saw of Drew he was dealing with consulate security.

At the hospital, she stood in the waiting room while Frost just sat in a plastic chair. He offered her no comfort, so she wrapped her arms around herself and paced.

She felt that terrible shrinking sensation again and a chill crawled along her skin. Suddenly the warmth of a suit jacket covered her shoulders. Allie turned to see Frost watching her closely.

"Time to sit down. You're going into shock. I want you to keep breathing normally."

But Allie couldn't seem to, she felt her world narrow to a pinprick as she looked at Frost, who swore softly.

He put his arms around her shoulders and led her to a chair, pushing her head between her knees.

"What's wrong with her?"

She heard Drew's voice but couldn't raise her head because Frost had his hand on the back of her neck.

"Aftershock," Frost said.

"Allie, breathe normally or you're going to pass out."

"That's no fun," she murmured.

"That's right, honey. No fun. You're okay now."

Frost let her go and she launched herself into Drew's arms.

Drew didn't give himself time to think about his own pain, his own needs. He couldn't stand by and watch Allie fall apart. He didn't have it in him to walk away. The love he never should have allowed to take root bound him there, drew him to her.

He gathered her close, cradling her against him as if she were made of crystal. He stroked her hair and kissed her temple and rocked her, crooning to her softly.

"Oh God, my cover's blown. I forgot to tell you. That man—Jammer. The Ghost's second-in-command. He knew I wasn't Callie…I mean, Gina. He kissed me and he knew."

"It's okay. You're out of it now."

"No, I'm not. I told him I was Tina, her twin sister. And I lied about where he could find Callie."

"Why?"

"He wanted to know. He insisted and I was so scared. Ohmigod, I couldn't take the chance he would hurt her."

"I don't think that's his motive, Allie. What would be the purpose? If he's willing to deal with you, he must want those guns pretty badly."

"When he let me go and when I came out of the room, that man pointed a gun at me. I think they were trying to kidnap me, not kill me, but Thad was there and he got shot."

"Any word on Thad?"

Frost shook his head and sat back in the chair. "He's in surgery is all I know. What's going on at the consulate?"

"I already called Director Santiago to get everything smoothed over. The Brits aren't happy about it, but they'll cover up the incident and keep everything confidential. Miyagi's people took out two consulate guards and did considerable damage to the building. They set the fire."

Frost asked, "Where are Leila and Jason?"

"They're making sure we weren't tailed."

Drew rubbed at the back of his neck and pulled Allie closer with his other arm.

When Leila and Jason walked through the hospital doors, Drew asked, "Any problems?" He was relieved that the rest of his team was safe. He pushed away the worry and focused on damage control.

"Couple of guys tried to follow. We took care of them."

Allie sat next to Drew, clutching Frost's tuxedo jacket around her with blood-stained hands.

He took her arm and steered her toward the unisex bathroom. Once inside he turned on the faucet and when the water was warm enough, he thrust her hands underneath. With the antibacterial soap, he started to clean away the blood.

Then he saw the blood on her thigh, dried in streaks down her leg. He lifted up the flimsy cloth of her dress.

"Allie, you're bleeding."

"I forgot. That man I hit. I think he cut me with a knife."

Drew led her out of the bathroom and found a nurse who directed him to a treatment room. Allie sat on the examining table while a doctor looked at the cut and told her she wouldn't need stitches. Just then, a nurse poked her head in and announced that there was a patient coming in who was critical, so the doctor pulled off his gloves and left the room.

Drew came over and bent down to examine the cut. The bastard had cut very close to her femoral artery, but the knife hadn't actually touched it. His heart lurched in his chest and a cold tingling sensation radiated out to his arms. She'd be okay, and he'd had men shot before—hell, he'd taken a bullet himself, but he'd never felt this kind of panic. Men, he reminded, men who'd made it part of their career choice, not some gorgeous interior designer who was an innocent target.

"It's not that bad," she said in a listless voice, not the bubbly voice he was used to. "I guess it'll be a battle wound. Do you think I'll get a purple heart?"

"This isn't funny, dammit. You shouldn't be in this situation or here with me." He opened a packet and dabbed at her cut.

"Ow, that stings." She looked him straight in the eye. "Let's not start that you're-not-a-bad-ass-secret-agent stuff right now. I'm carrying through on my part of the bargain and there isn't anything you can do about it, so live with it, Drew."

He couldn't help the smile twisting his lips, and he relaxed. She sounded a lot more like herself.

"I should have watched you more closely and then your shapely ass wouldn't have been in hot water tonight."

"It happened way too fast and I pulled my shapely ass out of the fire, thanks very much. I think Sydney Bristow would be so proud of me."

"This isn't a television show, Allie."

"Geez, you think?" Allie rolled her eyes. "You're in a bad mood."

He slathered ointment, then put a gauze pad over the cut and used tape to secure the bandage to her skin.

Yeah, he was in a bad mood, and he knew why. Seeing Thad go down had brought back too many memories of his last team and what had happened to them. Drew clenched his teeth. Didn't his father say never get involved? It only hurt when things changed. Yet, he knew that Thad, Leila and Frost were three of the best operatives. He was proud to work with them.

And the other reason he was on edge was Allie. He always worked alone when he was undercover, relying on himself, his intel and his skills. He could react to quick change in the plan. But Allie? He closed his eyes, facing a truth he'd tried to avoid. He was afraid for her and, dammit, afraid for himself. Walking away from Allie was going to be difficult, but at least he would know that she was getting on with her life. If it came to her death, it would haunt him for the rest of his life.

He went over to the sink and wet a pad and returned to the table. He squatted to wash the dried blood off her leg.

"Drew?" Allie said softly.

He looked up at her.

"Before I took this on, I didn't understand the danger. It was easy to say yes, but now I know what we're up against, it terrifies me. I won't lie. But I've got to see this through."

"You don't have anything to prove to anyone, Allie."

He gently slipped off her high-heeled sandal and continued to swab at the dried blood.

"Yes, I do. Maybe mostly to myself. My family doesn't really think much of me. They indulge my whims. That's what they call them. *Whims.* Callie was always the dutiful one. The one who made a difference. I just made people laugh."

"Laughter is a gift, Allie."

"They were laughing *at* me, Drew. Big difference there."

"Then they can't appreciate what they have. I think you're selling yourself short. My family didn't laugh much at all. We just moved from base to base."

"I'm sorry, that must have been hard." Her hand went into his hair, her fingers ruffling the strands. His scalp tingled where her fingers touched.

"No, it wasn't. If you don't get attached to anything, it's easy to pick up and leave."

He rose and threw the pad in the trash and turned back to her. Grasping her around the waist, he lifted her off the table.

"Surely you had friends." Her arms went around his neck and she pressed against him. The suit jacket slipped off her creamy shoulders and Drew caught it before it hit the floor.

He'd had friends in his early years, but as his family continued to move, he'd given up getting close to anyone. "Friendships need to be nurtured. I didn't get the time to do that. Soon, I stopped trying."

He settled the jacket more firmly around her shoulders and wrapped his arms around her.

"So this life you lead now isn't much different, is it?" She stared up at him, her eyes as bright as sapphires, as uncertain as a child's.

In spite of all she'd been through, an aura of innocence still clung about her like a fading perfume.

He shrugged, tenderly brushing her hair from her eyes. He grazed his fingertips along the delicate line of her cheekbone. "It suits me."

"Does it? Does it really suit you now or would you like something permanent?" she asked cautiously, studying him from beneath her lashes.

"Are you fishing?"

"No. I'm asking you a simple question."

Her expression was completely guileless. It's no wonder she couldn't have pulled off posing as Gina.

He pinned her with a look. "There is nothing simple about that question, Allie."

He drifted away from her and stood at the window, looking out into the dark. The wind had come up and bent the branches of the trees. Lightning flashed in the distance.

Drew spoke. "I told you from the beginning that I wasn't going to stick around for long."

She sighed. "That's right. You did. I didn't complain." Allie limped over to him, clutching at the jacket, and leaned her shoulder against the window.

"No. You didn't," he replied, "but I can hear it in your voice and unlike most men, I can read the subtext. You want me to hang around."

"So what if I do?" she said. "What would be so bad about that?"

He watched her blink quickly, as if she were afraid to take her eyes off him for even a fraction of a second. But she held her ground, brave and foolhardy to the last. And his heart squeezed painfully at the thought. She was waiting for a qualification, something that would dilute the truth into a more palatable mix.

"It's not the way I'm wired."

"Wires can cross."

He laughed softly. "You are funny, Allie. Your family's missing out."

She smiled at him. "It's possible to change things, Drew. Just because you've lived a certain way in the past doesn't mean you have to live that way always."

"No. I guess I don't, but I'd rather deal with the demons I know than the ones I don't."

"Coward."

He was amazed at the sting of that one word. "Maybe."

"I see the possibilities and you see the barriers. Maybe we *are* too hardwired to change."

"I wouldn't want you to change, Allie."

She stepped closer to him, her gaze never letting go of his. Her eyes were as wide and blue as heaven, reaching into him, touching places in his heart that hadn't been touched, ever. Calm and fearless, she whispered, "Okay, I'll leave that up to you."

He pulled her into his arms, unable to stand even the small space dividing them. He skimmed her jaw with his mouth, kissed the top of her head. "Don't expect me to change."

"I'll have all the expectations I want, Agent Miller. You can take that to the bank and get interest on it."

Frost walked in. "The surgeon's here. He says that Thad is going to be fine. He's still under now, but the doc says we can see him tomorrow."

"You all head home," Drew said.

When Drew came out of the treatment room, Jason was waiting for them.

"What are you still doing here?"

"I want to make sure Allie gets home. Do you have a problem with that?"

Drew could see the concern on Jason's face and shook his head.

Once back in the loft, Jason insisted on talking to Drew. While Allie went into the bathroom, Drew poured himself some whiskey from the small bar in the living room. He offered some to Jason, who shook his head.

"I can find Miyagi and take him out right now, Drew," Jason said. He paced in front of the large windows, backlit by the lightning far in the distant dark sky.

"Don't be stupid. That will only make matters worse. If Miyagi is killed by one of us, the yakuza will continue to hunt Gina to avenge him. It's a no-win situation."

"I don't give a damn about your mission! I care about Allie, and her life is in danger. We should do something about it, now!"

"We will. But not right now." He sat down in a chair and downed the contents of the glass in one swallow. It burned all the way to his gut.

"Tonight…"

"Tonight was about her inexperience. Thad got shot because she's not an agent."

The gasp made him look around. Allie stood just outside the bathroom door, her face pale. She limped to the living room with purpose in her broken stride.

12

"YOU BLAME ME," she said, horrified.

"Oh, hell." Drew stood reaching for her. "No, I don't. Of course not. It's your inexperience."

She backed away. "I know that I'm not spy material. Believe me, being threatened with both a knife and gun, getting sliced and seeing Thad shot makes me know I'll never score high on the Myers-Briggs in the Secret Agent category, but I did my best."

"Allie, I don't blame you." He tried to hold her, touch her, but she turned away from him, hugging herself.

"Thad's my friend, too, Drew." Her eyes filled with angry tears that never fell.

"I didn't mean that it was your fault that Thad got shot."

"It doesn't matter. I'm so used to it." She looked at him sharply. "I did the best I could." She limped away from him.

"Allie?"

"Don't talk to me," was all she said.

Drew dropped into the chair. *Damn. You can be a perfectly insensitive jerk sometimes.* Give him a tough situation and he could handle it without a problem, but Allie was a different kind of trouble. She'd just given him a wake-up call that maybe he'd been in the field far too long. He'd lost something of himself out there. He wanted it back.

"You're an ass," Jason blurted in disgust. "I think Allie pulled off almost the impossible while keeping us all alive and protecting her cover. She should get a medal if you ask me."

"Shut up!" Drew snarled, springing out of the chair.

"I think you don't want to look too closely at your own feelings." Jason got right into Drew's face.

Drew wanted to hit the punk, but instead he crowded him against the wall.

Jason went on, "You have feelings for her. You might as well admit it and go down in flames." He didn't flinch or budge an inch, but met Drew's glare with one of his own.

Drew backed up and swore. The whole situation was something he didn't want to deal with.

"I'm right, Drew. Deal with it or you'll be the one to get someone killed." Jason left, closing the door softly behind him.

If Drew was honest with himself, he would analyze his reaction. He would admit that Allie meant a lot to him. He would admit that he'd panicked when he couldn't find her, when he'd seen the blood on her. It was so clear to him that she was in over her head.

He reached for the phone and punched the numbers, his gaze on the bathroom door, willing her to come back out. She didn't.

Gillian answered on the first ring.

"More problems?" she asked before Drew could speak.

"Thad is out of surgery and will be fine. Allie was wounded with a knife, but she's also fine. We need to make it look like Callie is still in that French hospital for just a day. She lied about Callie's location to the Ghost's lackey."

"Done," Gillian said. "Anything else?"

"Allie's not cut out for this."

"She's done great so far. I'd say you're underestimating her. You might want to ask yourself why."

Drew ended the call. He could only concentrate on Allie, the pain in her expression, the blame she shouldered. He rubbed his eyes. *You single-minded ass,* he thought, and pulled out the picture he'd kept for a long time. The torn photo showed six men, all smiling, all in battle gear. Drew was front and center, Martinez beside him. He had thought that if he'd kept his distance, he wouldn't get caught up in any type of relationship.

But, Thad, Leila and Frost were not only his teammates, they were his friends. Even Jason Kyoto had proven himself and Drew couldn't help it—he liked the kid. He liked the kid a lot.

Jason was smart to tell Drew to examine his own feelings about Allie. Drew knew it was easier to force them back than to let them in, and he was so hard-pressed to get the mission done that he hadn't truly considered the emotional beating she'd endured. And he'd just twisted her guilt a bit deeper with his unthinking remark.

Drew pocketed the picture, then pushed back in the leather chair and stood.

Drew rapped on the bathroom door. She didn't answer. "Allie, I'm sorry."

"Whatever, Drew." Her voice was clearly clogged with tears.

Boy, he really needed to engage his brain before he engaged his vocal chords.

"I said those things to you because I was…" *Say it,* he urged himself. *Just say what you mean.*

She threw open the door, her eyes red and her face flushed. "You think I'm impressed by all this cloak-and-dagger crap? I'm not." She pushed past him into the hall, then stopped, delivered a wounded glare and said, "Finish your sentence."

"I was out of my mind with worry and panic. When I saw the blood on you, I wanted to…" The dark side of him wasn't a side he wanted her to see. But Allie wasn't some shallow blond bimbo. She wanted to know, but he was afraid to let go and expose her to the ugly side. Still, she deserved to know who he was, really know after all that she'd been through. She'd committed herself to this mission and bonded with his team. She cared deeply or else she wouldn't have been crying.

Intimacy was about baring something deep inside him, something hidden sometimes from himself. Locking her out would effectively drive her away.

"Please, Drew. Tell me." She bit her bottom lip, her eyes pleading.

It was more than he could take. His heart squeezed hard in his chest. "I don't want you in my world. Talking about it is just as bad."

"So you keep everything bottled up inside? Covert operations dictate you have to keep all your emotions undercover. What kind of way is that to live?"

He captured her eyes with his gaze, thinking, *if I don't cage her, she'll run from my words.* "You really want to know who I am? It will give you the same nightmares."

"No, it won't. I'm stronger than I look."

"I do what must be done, whatever it is, and I stay until

the job is done. Hell, I've been in and out of the U.S. so much I don't even own a home here. I got most of the scars on my body from an ambush when I was a Ranger along the Afghan/Pakistani border. Tough terrain, but the toughest problem is figuring out who to trust. Our Afghani guide was a Taliban agent and he led us to an ambush. We were pinned down in crossfire and every single one of my teammates died, including Ray Martinez. He was a close friend." It was the first time he'd said it and a knot released in his chest. "They left me for dead."

Allie wrapped her arms around Drew and squeezed. "Ohmigod." She absorbed his words, trying to take in his pain.

"I once promised to protect the citizens of this country in any way I possibly could. Even though I'm no longer in the military, I still embrace that oath."

His brutal honesty settled deep inside her. He was a man who found it difficult to admit to any weakness.

"I come from a military family, Allie. And the military came first in every way, including emotionally. My father taught me to withhold emotion for the people we met. For me, it became a badge of honor."

And that honor is what drove him now. Of course, he would see his inner fears and insecurities as inadequacies in himself.

"I'll do anything in my power to see the mission succeeds."

"You've done horrible things."

His face closed, his eyes shuttering. "I told you this wouldn't be pretty."

When he looked up at her she could see that he thought she was judging him. He dropped his arms, started to turn away.

"No, Drew." She wrapped her arms around his neck and pulled his rigid body against hers. "I wouldn't ever judge you." He was what she'd thought he was from the moment she'd met him. A warrior whose significance had got lost in the bigger issues, in the fight against evil and oppression. Allie now had the personal story of one such warrior, seeing firsthand what lengths he'd gone to and would continue to go to, to make a difference.

Stopping the Ghost would keep devastating weapons out of the hands of America's enemies. It represented one link in a very long chain that stretched all the way to Afghanistan and Iraq. Drew had given up everything to face that threat and defeat it. His courage alone was almost unfathomable.

He was self-sacrificing, but she was selfish enough to want him for herself.

He tried to pull away, but her arms tightened around him. "I'm not judging you," she repeated, "I'm not," she said when he tried to pull away again. "I'm just trying to understand all this. Trying to understand you. It's important to me."

He went still against her as if he couldn't believe what she was saying. Obviously he thought it was impossible for her to care about a man so deeply entrenched on the dark side. With a soft groan, he buried his face in the hollow between her neck and shoulder. "Allie, oh, Allie."

She wasn't really any different from him. She wanted to be accepted for who she was in light of all the things she'd done in her life. She moved away a bit so he would look at her. She cupped his face in her hands and slid her thumbs rhythmically along his cheekbones. "Everybody has secrets, Drew. Yours are safe with me."

Drew slammed his eyes shut, tipped his head back and,

for a moment, he held his breath. "Safe, sure, but accepted. What I've done…"

There was an odd catch in her voice as she moved her arms to his waist and laid her head on his chest. "Protect and defend—it's enough for me."

DREW BRUSHED a kiss on her cheek. "Enough." He squeezed her tightly, aching inside. He'd never trusted a woman enough to reveal even this much and he knew he never would again.

She pressed her face directly into his chest. It brought a smile and he was profoundly moved by the comfort she found before he found the same comfort in her. He pressed his mouth to the top of her head, rubbing her spine.

She let out a long sigh. "We'll seal it with a kiss."

He smiled slightly as his gaze traveled over her face, the fall of her hair, just noticing the dark flecks of midnight blue in her eyes. Her expression was at once innocent and sexy. A hell of a combination. Drew wasn't much on centerfold types; pretty was good, but most times after a couple of months he didn't like what he found beneath. With Allie, he already knew what lay beneath, aside from a zany sense of humor.

She pursed her lips and made kissing noises.

"One kiss? That's all? Sorry, that's not enough," he murmured, brushing her lips with his own.

"We can start with that. Who cares where we end up?"

His mouth captured hers on a breath of laughter that echoed in the high-ceilinged loft. Something he couldn't name fractured inside him. It wasn't immediate, it'd been there, dormant—in that place where he'd compressed most of his emotions—the need to connect to her when he'd been going solo for so long. He deepened the kiss and the wall inside him crumbled, releasing what was trapped there, and it howled free.

Allie felt a definite change in him. His mouth went from patience to possession, marking her as his, branding her with the fire of his need. He knew she'd deny him nothing of herself.

He was right.

His hands splayed against her back, driving up her spine as his warm mouth moved over hers with edgy desperation. She felt him tighten his control, beating back his desire to conquer and plunder. She lost all sense of time, her thoughts centered on only one thing. More. She wanted more with this man.

Drew gave. "You know where we're going." It wasn't a question.

Yet her answer spoke in her tongue sliding into his mouth, in her hips rising to mesh with his. Drew nearly roared, his control slipping another notch. His hands followed her contours, and she moaned a delectable, tiny sound that nearly tore through his fraying control.

Impatiently, he gripped her at the waist and lifted her to the table. She gasped as the cold wood hit the backs of her bare legs.

His mouth covered hers in a swoop of heat more frantic, more demanding.

She pulled away, ducked seductively, made him come after her with a growl. Drew felt strung out, manipulated by the strings she had on him. He let her play him. Her life was in danger and she wanted control, wanted to command something, and he let it be him. She nipped his neck; a hot, desperate need filtered down to his heels. He wanted her, right now, on the table, and the image made his dick harden like rock. When she broke the kiss, it was to peel off his shirt. Her hands scraped over his skin and she dragged her tongue across his nipple and then suckled.

It left him trembling, and he gripped her hips, wedging closer. His hand slid upward, over the silk covering her, along her ribs, teasing the underside of her breasts. Her kiss intensified.

His gaze roamed down her body, and everything between them seemed to go still for a moment. By increments she leaned closer, the soft material of her dress grazing his chest. Then she did that arching thing that was so amazing. She just lay back and he pulled the dress over her head and off her body.

The removal of the dress left her in nothing but a lacy, hot-pink bra and matching panties. He fought for patience when he was craving her like air, his body flexing with need.

He reached for the strap at one of her shoulders. "I want to see you."

He reached around her and undid the bra and pulled it off, dropping it on the floor.

His chest was inches away from her breasts. Allie was panting, the rise and fall of her nipples so close that it was torture. He leaned closer. That first press of flesh to flesh held a sort of euphoria, crossing the line of intimacy. Nothing in life compared to the single moment when you invited someone this close.

She was still, waiting for his touch, watching his hands come toward her and when they covered her breasts and kneaded the tender buds of her nipples, she covered his big hands and arched. Drew kissed her, loving her moans, her eagerness.

He wouldn't last long.

Not with her small hands clutching at his shoulders, sliding over his hair. He bent, his gaze locked with hers as he closed his lips around her nipple. She watched it, the erotic slip of his tongue over her flesh and he felt her muscles tighten.

Then he moved lower, across her stomach; carefully he spread her legs, moving between.

"You okay?"

"I won't be if you stop."

He held her gaze as his finger followed the edge of her inner thigh. He found her and her gasp lit him on fire as he stroked her. At eye level, he missed nothing. Her tight grip, the way her hips started to move with his hand, her scent.

She hung on. "Drew, damn you."

He thrust his fingers inside, and she came off the table, but he pushed her back till she lay flat, then his mouth was on her, tongue laving, and Allie shrieked and squirmed.

"Oh, damn. Damn that's good."

He flicked her clit, then circled it, over and over as his fingers slid in and out. He watched her writhe, draw her legs up and move her hips in a way that almost made him come. He wanted to be there, and he would be, yet Drew held her still, a testimony to his will when he wanted to slam into her and fuck her silly. But this was different. She was different.

She sat up and climaxed in his arms, clinging to him, her hips thrusting, her expression startled and so unlike any before. Transformed in ecstasy. A little wild, a little innocent. And he held her as she rode the wave of pleasure.

When she settled, went limp, Drew wrapped his arms

around her. Cupping her behind, he pulled her off the table. Her legs went around his waist and she met his gaze, blushing. He felt the heat of her through his pants as he walked, taking her where he wanted her. To the bed. He lowered her legs to the floor, and her hands splayed over his chest. Drew knew what people saw when they looked at him— a scarred warrior—but that wasn't the way Allie looked at him, admiration and desire shone in her eyes as she opened his pants wide.

She met his gaze, smiling smugly as her fingers dipped inside and enclosed him. He closed his eyes. His chest rose and fell hard.

"You really are the man of steel."

Hurriedly, he toed off his boots. "Maybe there, but my restraint is crumbling."

She took a long look, her hands following her gaze sliding over his cock. He groaned.

"You're making me insane," he said, pulling her hand free. She gave him free rein over her body. He took it, feeling the sleek turn of her hip, the soft warmth he wanted to enfold him. He insinuated his knee between her thighs, teasing her, rubbing and thrusting till she squirmed with need. Then he eased back, one knee on the bed to pick her up and place her in the center of the bed.

Allie grinned, watching him come closer. He reached across her and got what he needed out of the drawer, but before he could open the packet, she grabbed it out of his hands, pushed him back onto his haunches and straddled his thighs.

The heat of her sex burned him as she rolled the condom down. He smoothed his hand over her glorious hair and kissed her.

Anticipation rocketed through him as she eased his erection down, the tip teasing her sleek core. Drew gripped her hips, dragged her close and slid into her in one smooth stroke. Eyes locked, they both breathed hard.

Her nipples barely touched his chest, and he cupped her jaw with one hand, driving his fingers into her hair and tipping her head back. It was possession, pure and simple. When she rocked, his kiss deepened. His hand slid down to close over her breast, his thumb making lazy circles while his other hand guided her, urged her. She never broke eye contact, her body undulating with seductive movements.

Drew swallowed, glancing down to see himself disappear into her body. He fought for command, to keep words he probably shouldn't say from spilling, but planted deep inside her, his body wasn't listening. He leaned in, kissing her, easing her to her back. He withdrew and thrust, and Allie bowed beautifully beneath him. She begged him to come closer, but he'd crush her so he grasped the headboard, one hand under her hips, giving them quick motion.

"Oh, damn, harder! Faster!"

"If I go faster, I'll lose it faster."

"Who cares?"

It was the death knell to his restraint. A surge of energy and his hips pistoned. She met and matched, drew her knees up, planted her feet flat, taking him in. She whispered his name, what he was doing to her, how it made her feel—and her lusty words pushed him to the brink. Then he felt her tense, quicken, captivated as she reached between them to feel him slide wetly into her, then retreat. Her touch was heavy and bold, and he loved this side of her. Hidden under the proper professional, she was sexy and daring. A little brazen. Her soft flesh hardened around him, trapped him in a throbbing flex of feminine muscle and slick skin.

Drew wanted more, wanted to connect when he hadn't—wouldn't—allow himself to have more than casual and quick sex till the next call, the next mission. He laced his fingers with hers, trapping her, spread under him like a sacrifice. Hovering on stiff arms, he held her gaze. Waited for her to object.

She didn't. A tiny smile fluttering through her gasps. "Drew, I won't break."

His control completely severed, Drew cocked his leg and pushed, driving her across the bed, a wave of desire so strong moving through him it was like a roll of thunder. He muttered a plea and thrust and thrust, and yet she still took him, her hips rising to grind to his.

Her breath hitched. Pale innocence met seasoned and scarred. His possession was raw and savage. She came and held nothing back from him, whispering her satisfaction. A flex of twisted muscle and slick bodies meshed as his climax joined hers. And she felt it, accepted the power of him, the brutal honesty of the moment.

Drew threw his head back, suspended, the wild grip of her flesh wringing him. Splintered rapture shredded his composure, yet in the deep throes of release, he noticed things. Every inch of her skin, her little tremors, the flare of her bright eyes. "Damn, Allie," he whispered, whipping his arms around her, the last threads of passion dissolving under a slow, thick kiss.

He rolled to his side, gently pulling her injured leg across his, and watched her world come into focus. Her lashes swept up, her eyes soft and feline-sexy. Her lips curved gently and Drew felt air lock in his lungs. Flushed and rosy, she was incredibly beautiful right then.

Breathtaking.

Needing to touch her again, he brushed her hair back, tucking it in behind her ear.

"Being a bad girl feels so very good. I sure hope you have more condoms in that drawer."

His smile was slow, and then he laughed. "I bought the economy pack."

13

THE DAY OF THE meeting with The Ghost, Allie paced, running her fingers through her hair. The cut on her leg was stiff and a little sore this morning thanks to the romping she'd done with Drew last night.

She stopped by the big windows as Katie's voice came back on the line.

"Sorry, it's been absolutely nuts here, Ms. Carpenter. Mr. Rosemont's custom-made armoire is finished ahead of schedule and the craftsman wants payment. He said he could deliver tomorrow. Mrs. Jamison has been calling every day and is thrilled with what you did with her sunroom. She wants you to do her whole vacation house out in Carmel and there are two friends who are members of her garden club who must have you do their homes. She told me to make sure to tell you that you're an absolute genius. And Lily Walden called. Ten times. She's simply frantic. She says her party is tonight and the decorating isn't done. I think she's the priority. I've not been able to reach Mr. Kyoto. I understand you had something personal to do, but it's not like Mr. Kyoto not to show up."

"Katie. Take a breath, hon. I'll try to get hold of Jason." Allie worried her lower lip. Would Jason be willing to help her out? He sure didn't have to pose as a decorator's assistant anymore. Where was Jason, anyway?

"I've alreay prepaid the craftsman for Mr. Rosemont's armoire. Please make arrangements to get it delivered to him today, if possible."

"You want me to supervise?"

"Yes. You can do it, Katie. I have faith in you and I'm so strapped for time."

"All right. Anything else?"

"Yes. Call back Mrs. Jamison and thank her for the compliment. I like being called a genius. Make an appointment with her for next week along with her two friends."

"Separate appointments?"

"Yes, make them separate."

"What about Lily Walden?"

"Leave her to me. I'll finish the decorating today and she'll be all set for her party tonight."

"Okay. I'll do it."

"Thanks, Katie."

"Is there anything else you need me to do?"

"No. There isn't." Allie looked toward the bed and the gorgeous sleeping man in it. "I just have one hell of a freaking obstacle to overcome. But I'm a genius, so I'll figure it out."

Drew will be reasonable, she thought as she closed her cell phone and made her way to the bed. Lily Walden *was* a big priority, and not following through on her job would hurt the success of Allie's decorating business.

Katie's call had woken her from a dreamless sleep in Drew's arms.

The events that had happened during the meeting with

Jammer at the consulate seemed like a terrible nightmare. The thought that she could have failed Drew last night settled into her mind and wouldn't let go.

Could she have prevented Thad from getting shot? Was it her woeful ineptness at this undercover-covert thing that had risked his life? All that vibrancy and optimism silenced forever. It hurt her heart to think about a world without Thad Michaels in it.

And it broke her heart to think of her life without Drew. But he'd made it perfectly clear in the hospital yesterday that once this mission was over, he would leave.

Well, right now he was here, and he was warm and hard in all the right places. She tucked her phone back in her purse and stared down at him.

Reaching out, she delved her fingers through his dark thick hair. His chest rose and fell rhythmically. The sheet was tangled around one heavily muscled thigh, leaving one half of his tight buttocks bare along with his hip, waist and rib cage. The strength of him was evident in all that tight, hard muscle. But it didn't show the intelligence that shone out of his deep blue eyes, or the compassion that he tried to hide. The way he had treated her yesterday after she'd blamed herself for Thad getting shot was something that she hadn't really expected.

Drew was the real deal. A real man with all the complexity of one. A man who put his life on the line to make his country safe.

She loved him.

That wasn't complex or puzzling.

It just was.

She loved him, and the pain of knowing that she wouldn't have many more of these moments just to stare at him almost made her want to walk out the door now. To do it before he became an overwhelming ache that never went away.

But she couldn't. She wanted everything, even that last tortuous second when he'd turn away and leave.

His hand snaked out and grabbed her around the waist. The suddenness of it made her shriek, but she laughed when she found herself sprawled across the hard muscled body she'd just been admiring.

"Are you ogling me in my sleep?"

"I don't ogle. It's unladylike."

"You were ogling. I felt your eyes on me."

"Okay, sue me. I was ogling."

He opened his eyes and she was trapped by the life she saw in them. So full and overflowing.

He held her gaze, laying a positively wicked smile on her, and Allie experienced it as if he'd held her heart in his palm. "If I sue, it won't be for money."

"Oh, no? What then?" She blinked, her eyes all innocence. "Surely, you couldn't have designs on my body?" She gasped in mock surprise. "Agent Miller, that's so wicked."

He laughed. "Designs, hell. I have full architectural renderings."

"I'm sure you know where all your *columns* are supposed to go." Cradled on his lap, she ran her finger over his collarbone, brushing at the knife wound halfway down his torso.

He groaned when she moved her pelvis against his. "One particular *column* needs to be placed just perfectly for maximum effect."

She laughed. "Really? Where could that be?"

He growled and flipped her onto her back. Her hands smoothed over his bare chest, her mouth was on his throat and trailing lower. "We're talking too much," she said, sliding her tongue over his nipple and hearing air hiss through his teeth. She liked that he tried to restrain himself. She nipped at his rib cage. His muscles jumped, and, when her hand traveled lower, Drew gripped her shoulders then rose above her.

"Before this gets too out of control, why don't you tell me what that phone call was all about, genius?"

"Killjoy." She taunted him with another heart-pounding kiss, then eased back. "I thought you were asleep."

"Covert operatives never sleep. We had sleep removed from our makeup," Drew deadpanned.

"Ha-ha."

"Were you going to ply me with sex and get me all weak and quivering before you told me of your decorating emergency?" Drew asked.

"You're so smart, aren't you? You're the freaking genius." Allie smiled. "You're never weak and quivering, even when you're hot for me."

His eyes danced with a snappy comeback, but instead, he leaned close and rubbed his mouth over hers. *What a guy,* she thought, and she felt a little bit of shame for trying to manipulate him. It didn't matter now, and Allie snuggled closer, staring up into his sharp eyes.

He chuckled and looked at her. Allie touched his face, pulled him down on her and he rolled with her to his side, drawing her leg over his. For a long moment they just stared at each other.

"I need to finish Lily Walden's home by tonight."

"Not going to happen."

"Don't act like this is *Mission Impossible,* Drew. It'll just be a few hours."

"Isn't that what you told Thad?" He raised one dark brow.

Allie giggled. "So, I miscalculated. What do we have to do but wait? I'm not really good at that, Drew. The more I think about what I have to do tonight, the more nervous I'll be. This will be a perfect outlet for my energy."

"Allie, it's just not a good idea to…"

"Please, Drew. I'm scared."

"Allie, don't… You're safe."

"No, I'm not talking about the physical danger, although that's very scary. After yesterday, I'm afraid more people will get hurt. Leila, Jason, Frost…you. I don't want to fail."

"You won't fail."

"No, you don't understand. Not the mission. You. I don't want to fail you. I've realized that I've never followed through with one thing I've tried in my life. That's why my family doesn't trust that I'll make a success out of this business. I've been a hot-dog vendor, sold catalog jewelry, been a waitress and worked retail. I failed because I never gave it my all. The design business is the most fun I've ever had in my life. I can see myself doing this forever. I don't want to let Lily down, not because of what my family will think of me, but because I'm dedicated to this one-hundred-percent."

His expression softened and he gently cupped her face in his palm. "How can I tell you no?"

"I hope she loves the job I do and I hope you also love the job I do."

"You'll do fine. Trust me."

"I do."

He smiled, blushing a bit, and she almost expected him to say something smart, and then knew he wouldn't. This was too important to belittle. He was that kind of man, sensitive yet jumping in with both barrels blazing, danger be damned. At least she knew to be scared about getting hurt when he left, she thought, her gaze sliding over his bare chest, his hair mussed from sleep, the dark stubble making him look every inch the dangerous male that he was. A definite threat to her libido. Could he be any sexier?

"You're one top-notch guy, Drew."

He smiled gently.

"I have to admit, in my ho-hum life I didn't know what it meant to have courage. I'm not just talking about taking me on, training me."

"Give yourself some credit."

"For trouble with a capital *T*." She pushed his hair back off his forehead. He had *hero* ingrained in every pore of his body, she thought. "Doesn't any of it scare you?"

Drew stared into her eyes and said, "Only you scare me."

"Why?"

"You do things to me."

Her lips curved. "Screw up your mission, get Thad shot, force you into decorating 101?"

"I'll admit the decorating was terrifying." He leaned in.

Allie felt swallowed up by the look in his eyes. Intense, for sure, but something else she'd never seen in a man. "Unconditional acceptance, huh?"

"And surrender," he murmured.

Tears blurred her vision and she inhaled sharply, a perilous feeling tumbling through her. "That's a low blow, especially when I'm trying to get something out of you," she whispered, touching the side of his face.

"You fascinate the hell out of me."

She smiled softly, a tear falling.

"Don't cry, Allie. I'd rather face an army. It shreds me."

"Are we shifting our focus from me to you now?"

He sighed heavily, "I can't deny you anything, it seems."

"Physically impossible, especially when the heat of you is burning me up."

Drew swore softly. "It's more than that and you know it." His fingers flexed on her jaw, something warring in his eyes.

Allie went still inside, and could have sworn her heartbeat just plain stopped. Was he authentic? No one had ever spoken to her like this. She cupped her palm over his hand. "Drew?"

"I mean it."

"I feel the same way." Her gaze lingered over him, her hand spread over his bare chest, the contours of muscle defined and rippling. It made her hot to see all of that man, and know he was hers for now. She lifted her gaze to his as she tugged at her robe's sash. She might have lost her wild edge along the way, but she wasn't shy. She went after what she wanted.

He covered her hand. "As much as I want to right now, I think we need to talk some more."

"But why waste this?" she said softly, reaching down and wrapping her hand around his rock-hard cock.

He elongated and flexed against her fingers; he groaned deep in his throat. "Allie—"

"Drew, please. I don't want to talk anymore."

"Nothing's resolved. How long do you think Lily Walden's job will take?"

"Six hours, tops."

He groaned, but this time it had nothing to do with desire.

"It would go faster if we had help."

"Who did you have in mind?"

"Jason, Frost and Leila. If they can shoot guns and run down bad guys, they can hang curtains and move around some furniture. We'll coin a new phrase in the decorating lexicon."

"What's that?"

"*Commando* Decorating 101."

"How did you get into this stuff anyway?"

She sighed. "Do you really want to hear this? Right now?"

"Yes. Right now."

Allie bit her lip. He was saying they might not have time later. "Okay, you win. When I was a girl, I played with my dolls like everyone else. And one Christmas, I got a dollhouse. It was a beautiful three-level Victorian. My grandfather built it for me. I spent countless hours playing with this beautiful house, spending my allowance on furniture. I would spend a lot of my waking time rearranging the furniture, coloring the walls, hanging clippings from my mother's magazines for artwork, or creating new ideas for tomorrow's play. Later in life, when I realized there was a profession that would allow me to do this for a living with real furniture and homes…"

"You knew you were on to something big."

"Uh-huh. Just like I know I'm on to something big here." She reached down and cupped him, the heat of his sex too hard to ignore against her flesh. "Can't we talk about this later?"

"I think you've settled it." He hissed in a breath when she moved her hand up his shaft and rubbed her palm around the tip. "We visit Thad first then…ah, damn, that feels good…then the…damn, Allie…the…ahhhh…."

"You're breaking up, Captain. My earpiece must be faulty."

"There's nothing faulty with your trigger finger."

"I need my whole hand to hold on to this weapon, and maybe my mouth and my tongue."

Pure heat and wild hunger ignited in his eyes. She loved that about him, the danger, the threat of pleasure she saw there.

Her free hand went to his neck and she drew him close. Her tongue snaked out and slicked his lips and he groaned.

She moved her hand again, slowly, seductively, loving the feel of his hard cock in her hand, and he groaned again.

His hands swept up her tight ribs, caressing her breasts. The contact was electric. His kiss stronger, hurried, he thumbed her nipples in slow circles, and her shudder tumbled into his mouth. Her strong thighs clamped him and he broke the kiss and held her gaze as he bent her backward over his arm and closed his lips over her nipple.

She stretched, moaning at the hot, wet heat of his mouth sliding over her skin. She watched as he took her flesh hungrily. "That is so erotic, Drew."

He smiled against her skin, lifting her higher against him, his tongue sliding over her breasts, his teeth deliciously scoring the plump underside. It wasn't enough. "Drew, inside please."

"Nope."

"You really are being a killjoy."

"Yes, ma'am."

She ran her hands down the hard muscles of his back over his firm butt. "So much of you is so big and strong. You feel so amazing, so wonderful."

"Too rough. Too many scars."

"I don't think so," she said quietly. "Nice and soft here," she said, running her palms up the inside of his inner thigh.

"And here," she said, kissing the smooth skin of his stomach. "And most definitely here," she said, running her tongue over the tip of his shaft. He flinched when she closed her hand over the base of his erection.

"You've, ah, proven your point…Allie."

Her mouth was on him, taking him deep. He couldn't tolerate it for long and she knew he was close. Allie loved it.

He took her down to the mattress, his hands and mouth trailing over her throat, her breasts. He paused to suck her nipples, draw on her skin, taste the curves of her ribs. His hands were busy everywhere, and Allie knew Drew had more skills than pulling a trigger and wielding a knife. Then he spread her thighs over his, baring her completely and met her gaze.

"No pithy comments?"

"Nope. Just a question. What are you waiting for?"

He laughed and his hands roamed from her knees to her center. He parted her, his fingertips dipping lightly, and he smiled as she twisted on the sheet, drew her knees up a bit. Pressing a finger inside her, he had her arching and thrusting into his touch.

"Oh, damn, again." He obliged. She squeezed her breasts, arched deeper and slid her hands down her thighs. "Now, please."

"No." He introduced another finger and stroked her.

She whimpered, but Drew refused to move faster, and she found out he was good at something else. Sheer torture.

Then she couldn't think at all as his tongue snaked and her breath hissed. He laid his mouth over her center, fingers peeling her wider as his tongue slicked in and out wetly. "Nothing to say now?"

"I am speechless," she gasped, and he lifted her hips, his tongue flicking and circling fast, then slow. Allie gripped her thighs.

He tasted her again and again, drawing her to the edge and letting her dangle. She bucked once, then twice and kept her hands on her breasts, her feet on the mattress and pushing.

"Please, Drew."

He arrowed up her body, pulling the nightstand drawer so hard it came out with a cracking sound. They both laughed like fools as he grabbed condoms until he could get one opened and cover himself.

Positioning himself, he grabbed the headboard and pushed into her. He left her completely and slid back, loving the look in her eyes as she watched his control snap like a dry twig.

Allie tangled her hands in his dark hair and moved restlessly beneath him. Wild sounds of yearning keening in her throat. She wrapped her legs around him, lifting her hips against his belly, seeking more contact, seeking to assuage the urgent ache that burned at the core of her desire.

"Oh, Drew." She gulped a breath and strained against the fist of desire that tightened and tightened each time he entered her.

His chest was heaving, his thrusts deeper, driving, straining, filling her to bursting. The time for play had faded, paled in the face of something hot and intense that enveloped them and threatened to consume them.

He withdrew fully and plunged, but she wanted more and harder and told him so, and he pumped. Her climax clawed through her body, wringing a long, hard moan out of her and, as it crested, Drew came with her on the tail end of her ride. His body twisted in ecstasy.

She wrapped her arms around his neck as he collapsed on top of her, his weight bearing her deep into the mattress. It was just what she needed, just when she needed it.

"Drew. You're freaking good."

"You make it so easy to be good, sweetheart."

He rolled onto his side and drew Allie with him. "It's getting late and we have a lot to do."

"Ah, recess is over, huh?"

Much later, as Allie sat on the bed getting dressed, Drew came out of the bathroom, a towel around his waist and one around his neck. His hair was damp and curling on the ends, something she found so endearing. He'd shaved.

He gripped the towel around his neck and she breathed deeply at how sexy he was standing there.

"This is a first. You're almost ready before me," he said.

"I get to wear my own clothes today." All she had left to do was slip on her jeans. "It's easier for me to decide what to wear. We have so much to do today, I didn't want to waste any more time."

"Hell, honey, that wasn't wasting time, that was making time."

She laughed. "Okay, you win."

He walked over to his closet and pulled out a pair of black jeans and a T-shirt with lettering that read West Point U.S.M.A on the front.

Allie examined the cut on her leg. It was still raw and red.

"How is it?" Drew came over to the bed and examined it himself.

"Hurts like a bitch."

"It's going to be your first scar."

"And hopefully my last. It was so damn scary."

"I'll be there every step of the way from now on. No more meetings with the Ghost alone."

"Thanks. He's in love with Callie and I was lucky to come in second best." *As usual,* she thought.

"Don't underestimate yourself."

"I know who I am, Drew. I know what people think of me."

"I don't think you do. You did something amazing."

"Then I think I deserve a reward." She gripped handfuls of his shirt and yanked. Her mouth melted into his and she took her time kissing him.

Even though they'd just fooled around, she wanted to have him again, nuzzle his neck, lick his skin. She sighed.

"How was that?" he asked when they parted.

"Better than Disneyland and Sea World combined."

"That good?"

"Yes."

He dropped the towel and slipped on white boxer briefs. The T-shirt quickly followed, then he slipped into the jeans and zipped and buttoned them.

"Are you ready to go?"

"Yes."

"Then let's go get that decorating done. If I know Thad, he's seduced every nurse in that place and is champing at the bit to get out of there."

"I'm just so glad he's going to be okay."

"Me, too. He's a good man."

"And I want to hear how he saved the President's life."

Drew chuckled as they left the loft.

HE DROPPED the receiver for the hundredth time. He could not go to France, not until this buy was over and Miyagi was taken care of. The news was all over the TV. They were reporting the fire at the consulate yesterday evening, but there was no talk of gunfire or any fatalities. He breathed easier. He wouldn't want to explain to Gina how he had let her sister die.

Her sister. Damn, the woman looked just like Gina right down to the color of her eyes. Yet the moment he'd gotten her in his arms, he'd known she wasn't Gina.

It had crossed his mind that it could have been some kind of trap, but no one except a twin could look that authentic, and she intended to go through with the buy. He needed the military weapons for Fuentes.

It was time to take the next step in his plan to cage and end the reign of Fuentes, one of the most dangerous drug kingpins in the world.

It was his destiny.

He moved away from the phone and the temptation. France and Gina would have to wait.

She was in a coma.

His beautiful Gina.

An uncontrollable restlessness had been brewing since last night. Since he'd heard the words come out of Tina's mouth.

His Gina with the light of the world in her eyes would recover, but that didn't alleviate the rage at Miyagi for trying to kill her.

Clutching his hands over his head, he howled his rage and his pain up at the plaster medallion on the ceiling.

Why? He wanted nothing from anyone, had done his best to avoid emotional entanglement. Yet here he was, in it up to his ears. The frustration of it hardened and trembled inside him. Eyes wild, chest heaving, he sat down heavily in his chair.

It should have been just a one-night stand, but it had evolved into something else over those three days.

The anger that had cloaked him had left him feeling naked and vulnerable, his heart pumping too hard in his chest.

He was such a fool.

He'd known it couldn't last and he'd been stupid to prolong it. They were both in a deadly business and she wasn't an angel even though she looked like one. He shouldn't want her, shouldn't try to be her champion, her knight in shining armor. He was a jaded mercenary, a man with ghosts.

He held his breath a moment, fighting the rise of the old bitterness he'd thought he'd conquered.

Hitting an intercom button, he spoke into the machine, addressing one of the men he'd hired. "Is Miyagi here?"

"Yes, sir. He just arrived."

"Send him up."

Fudo Miyagi stepped through the door that his associate held for him. Jammer sat behind his desk. The Japanese yakuza scanned the room, nodding at the show of wealth and the seat of power. He started across the room and when he reached the desk, he bowed.

Jammer didn't return the courtesy. He gestured toward one of the leather chairs. Miyagi's wrinkled face frowned, his brown eyes snapping.

He sat. Jammer had had no doubt that he would. When he'd contacted Miyagi, he'd hinted that he had very important information Miyagi would want.

"I understand that you're looking for someone. Gina Callahan."

Miyagi's eyes widened and he leaned forward. "You have information on this woman?"

"Yes, I do."

"I am not a patient man."

"I want the rocket-propelled grenades you have in your possession. It's a big shipment and I need it for a client."

"That shipment has been promised to another client."

"That's too bad. We're done here."

Miyagi sat still for a minute. "I agree. Where can I find the Callahan woman? She has humiliated me and damaged my reputation. I must have retribution."

"As a matter of fact, she'll be there tonight when we exchange the merchandise—The Port of Los Angeles, Berth 271."

14

ONCE AT the Walden Estate, Allie made a game plan to finish the rest of the house. They stopped first at the wooden gate flanked by stone posts, and Allie made sure it was left open so that all the delivery trucks could get through. Once through, they climbed the driveway to the house.

Just as they were all entering the estate through the front door, Allie's cell rang. When she answered and listened, her face fell. "Oh, no. No. I understand."

"What is it?" Jason asked.

"My carpenter's had a family emergency and can't work today."

"What do you need done, luv?" Frost asked.

"Carpentry work mostly, assembling a headboard, putting up curtain hardware and making a cabinet to go in the dining room."

"Show me the power tools and your plans and I'll get started."

At her incredulous look, Frost chuckled. "I wasn't always a mercenary, Allie. My da was a carpenter and he taught me everything he knew."

"I can't believe my good fortune. You all can do just about anything."

"What room did you want to start in first?"

"Jason, dining room. Those walls need to be covered and it looks like the first of the deliveries is here."

"I'll take care of the truck and then get started on the room."

"I'll help," Leila offered, following Jason out the front door to the truck.

Allie set down her bag on a foyer table and pulled it open, extracting her plans. "Here are the drawings and the dimensions. The wood is in the garage along with the tools. I need the headboard frame asap."

Frost nodded and took the paper and walked away.

"Drew, you and I have to go to the library first. I need that sofa moved up to the bedroom. I found tapestry material to match and I'm going to make the headboard out of it. I also found these great art deco lamps and figurines… Oh, shoot. I left them at the office."

"Want me to go get them?"

"No. I can have Katie bring them here."

Allie called and talked to her secretary.

"Let's go get that sofa."

Drew and Allie brought the small sofa up the stairs to the master suite.

"Where's Lily?"

"She's staying in downtown LA at her mother's town-house while I get the rest of the house done."

"This is a pretty big job for you."

"Well, you've been a big help. You know, you have a knack for it, I think."

Frost came through the door with the frame for the head-board and there was no more time for talk. Jason arrived to help Allie stretch the material and staple it to the frame.

When that was over, Allie sewed rust-colored buttons all over the fabric.

They placed the sofa and made up the bed and the master suite was done.

All of them headed downstairs, and the doorbell rang as they hit the bottom.

When Frost opened the door, Katie, Allie's secretary, stood there, juggling two lamps and a box. Frost caught the lamps and then Katie's eyes met his. Allie watched as Damian Frost got lost in Katie's brown eyes. Katie, on the other hand, just stood there like a deer in the headlights.

"Katie, thanks for bringing this stuff by. I really appreciate it." Allie engaged the girl in conversation about the Rosemont armoire, but Katie kept giving Frost clandestine looks.

Frost set the lamps down by the door and turned away, but not before Allie saw the longing on his face, quickly masked. If Allie hadn't been looking straight at him, she probably would have missed it.

Katie left and Allie was on the move again. The dining room was completed in an hour.

It was five o'clock when they finished. Lily had returned and the flower people were already unloading the table arrangements. As they got in the car, the caterers pulled up.

ONCE Allie and Drew returned to the loft, he needed little time to change into all-black clothes, and arrange an array of firepower on the dining-room table.

"Hey, looks like we're going to a war." She tried to sound flippant, but her voice came out weak.

"Just getting everything ready for tonight. We pick up

the gun shipment in an hour. Your training is over. All of this is almost over."

Allie nodded and went to Gina's suitcase. Now what would her sister wear to a war? Her hands shook as she reached down and pulled out a pair of black leggings, a tight, hot-pink top and the boots she'd worn to Hell and Gone. They made her feel powerful. Right, powerful.

Actually, right now her bones felt as if they'd turned into jelly. Suddenly a warm hand landed on her shoulder and his presence anchored her. Drew.

"I'll be with you every step of the way. I promise. We're not going to let anything happen to you. You start off the buy and we'll finish it. The Ghost goes down tonight."

Allie nodded. She went to change.

It wasn't long before they were speeding down the freeway toward the Port of Los Angeles located in San Pedro Bay, just twenty miles south of downtown Los Angeles. Frost drove the truck packed with weapons with Leila riding shotgun and Jason followed on his flashy motorcycle. The closer they drew to the port the more Allie's nerves seemed to overtake her.

By the time they pulled up to Berth 271, she was shaking. Remembering what had happened at the consulate sent fear and adrenaline into her system. She wanted to bolt from the vehicle and run.

When Drew put his hand on her arm, she jumped. He grabbed her chin and his concerned eyes took in her face. "Allie…"

"I can't do it. I can't. I'm sorry, but I'm so out of my league here. I'm scared down to my toenails. I'm afraid I'll mess it up and get someone else shot or worse."

"It's okay, Allie. Calm down. I could go in there and tell

Jammer that your sister took a turn for the worse and you've gone to be by her side. Let you stay in the car and stay low. But, I need you in there."

Allie tried to get hold of herself, but the thought of all those weapons, the terror she'd lived through at the consulate, all took her by surprise. Clear, linear thought was beyond her. Drew spoke again.

"I'll be the first to admit when I'm wrong, but at every step of this mission, you've been there one-hundred-percent. Quick thinking on your part saved this job."

"I just can't."

Drew nodded and got out of the car.

She'd failed again. It was her destiny to be a coward and not follow through. All those years in the shadow of her sister had made Allie afraid of moving out of it and trying something on her own. Here she was, poised on the edge of doing something spectacular, and she was too damned scared to get out of the car.

Drew needed her.

Somewhere inside she found the courage to grip the door handle and open it. She stepped out and ran toward the big double doors of the warehouse. When she was almost there, she stopped, gathered her composure and swung her hips as nonchalantly as she could manage. *Don't act like Gina, be Gina.*

Once she cleared the doors, she heard Jammer demand, "Where's Gina?"

"She's right here," Allie said loudly, before Drew could give Jammer the excuse he'd come up with in the car. "Where's the Ghost? You said he'd be here."

"He is. He's upstairs in the office."

They looked up to see a silhouette in the curtained window. A voice came over the loudspeaker. "Jammer, make the deal and let's get out of here."

Jammer opened a briefcase on a nearby table situated near the door. Allie schooled her features at the amount of money in the case. She nodded and smiled at Jammer.

"The guns are in the truck."

Drew stayed close to Allie, but Leila and Frost went to the truck to open the doors so Jammer could inspect the merchandise. After looking at one of the AK-47 machine guns, he ordered two of his men to load them onto a waiting boat.

Something metallic-sounding hit the cement floor of the warehouse.

Before he knocked her to the ground, Allie heard Drew shout, "Flash grenade!" Then her head contacted the concrete and she blacked out.

MAX CARPENTER stretched his legs and leaned back in his chair. The San Pedro Branch of the FBI was quiet. Max had just finished his paperwork on a serial killer that he and his partner had recently caught.

His phone rang.

"FBI."

"There's an arms deal going down tonight. Your sister is involved. Military weapons, rocket-propelled grenades, the Ghost and Fudo Miyagi."

"Who is this?"

"Go to the Port of Los Angeles, Berth 271."

"Who is this?" he asked again, but the line went dead.

ALLIE WOKE with a pounding headache and her throat felt raw. When she groaned, someone grabbed her by the hair and jerked her head up.

"Tell me where she is, Ms. Callahan, and I'll let you live."

Allie opened her eyes to find Drew, Frost, Leila and Jammer and his men all kneeling on the concrete warehouse floor.

For a moment the heavily accented English didn't penetrate.

"Who?"

"Mr. Kyoto's sister."

Jammer interjected, "This was not our deal, Miyagi."

Miyagi nodded and the man standing next to Jammer shoved Jammer across the chest.

"Mr. Kyoto's sister, Ms. Callahan."

"Not going to happen," Allie said through gritted teeth, the burning pain in her scalp making her breathless.

Miyagi pulled her to her feet and she heard Jammer repeat, "This wasn't our deal, Miyagi."

"Go upstairs and bring the Ghost down here," he ordered as one of his men prodded Jammer in the back. Jammer moved up the stairs, but it wasn't long before Miyagi's thug came rolling down the stairs.

Miyagi pulled Allie up by her hair. Drew's training rang in her head. *Always look for a way out.*

There was a stairway guarded by two men and a door that looked as if it led to a room. To the far side of the warehouse there was plenty of cover. She had to do something.

Drew's eyes were locked to hers and she wanted to shout his name. No one moved. In the silence Allie heard the heavy beat of a helicopter overhead.

"Looks like the Ghost has an alternative plan." Miyagi cackled. "I'm going to make you pay before I cut out your heart. You'll beg for death." He ground the gun he held in his hand against Allie's temple.

"No!" Drew roared, and Miyagi turned toward the sound.

"Ah, the man in the hospital wasn't yours. Is this your man? I will take him from you."

The gun was gone from her head and Allie didn't hesitate. With all her strength, she used her fist to hit Miyagi as hard as she could in the groin. Miyagi's shot went wild and he crumpled.

A shout from the open door to the warehouse startled everyone. "FBI. Freeze." And all hell broke loose as a burst of automatic fire tore up the warehouse walls.

Allie ran for the stairs, thinking she might detain the Ghost. Before she reached the first riser, Miyagi was there with a knife to her throat.

He dragged her up the stairs.

Drew followed, understanding in a heartbeat what Allie had been trying to do.

He took the stairs two at a time and hit the door at the top with his shoulder, breaking through. He ran full-out, his only thought to get to the roof.

He gained the roof, but Miyagi was already halfway across. He was going to take Jammer's helicopter.

Then, once again, Allie did something totally unexpected, something Drew wouldn't have expected a novice operative to do. She went down, just went limp as a wet noodle. Miyagi staggered under her weight and had to let her go to brace himself against the asphalt of the roof.

Drew shot the knife out of his hand. Miyagi clutched his hand and turned to run for the chopper. But he never got inside—a booted foot sent him careening back.

The chopper took off and Drew saw Jammer's face in the glass. He saluted.

Miyagi recovered quickly and ran at Drew like a

wounded bear. With quick jabs and flying fists, Drew met Miyagi head-on.

Miyagi wasted no time and went after Drew's vital zones, but Drew blocked every move. With rapid punches, Miyagi delivered a blow to Drew's midsection that had him grunting and landing on his back. Miyagi tried to bring his foot down on Drew's head, but Drew rolled out of the way and got back onto his feet.

He shot out a jab of his own that Miyagi blocked. Drew immediately went for his knee and threw him to the ground.

Miyagi rose and looked around frantically. He ran for the edge of the roof and the fire escape. Allie was up and running, too.

"No!" Drew yelled, but it was too late. Allie caught up to Miyagi and threw herself at him. He went down and slid right over the edge of the roof. Allie couldn't let go in time and she began to slide over with him.

Drew jumped forward, landing on his stomach just as Miyagi went over. Allie screamed, but Drew managed to grab hold of her shirt, stopping her momentum.

He held her in midair and crawled back inch by inch, her weight pulling on his shoulder, but he had no intention of letting her go.

"Drew," she said softly.

"Hang on, Tinkerbell. I've got you."

Drew heard pounding feet and turned to look over his shoulder. What he saw wasn't good. It was one of Miyagi's men and he wasn't going to be happy to see his boss sprawled on the sidewalk below.

"Allie, hang on," Drew said as he set her hands on the edge of the roof and rolled to get his gun.

When he got his hand on the grip, he reached out and

pulled the trigger in successive bursts. The gunfire hit the guy in the chest and he went down.

Allie began to slip and Drew dropped the gun and hauled her up into his arms.

For a moment he just sat there holding her.

"Thanks," she said over and over. "Thank you so much."

"Hands up," a voice said, and Drew turned to see a man with a gun pointed at him. Drew breathed a sigh of relief when he noticed the man's jacket was emblazoned with the white letters, FBI.

Allie raised her face from Drew's shoulder.

"Max?" she said.

THEY WERE all taken into custody to keep Gina's cover intact, but the sting operation to capture the Ghost was a bust. Inside the upstairs room, they found a cardboard cutout anchored to the window and a taped recording of the Ghost's voice rigged to the loudspeaker. Jammer was long gone with the military weapons, the launchers and all of Miyagi's money. The guy was slick.

Allie had a lot of explaining to do, and Max pulled her and Drew into an interrogation room at the Westwood Building to hear every word. To say he was mad was an understatement.

When he let her go with a lecture, they emerged from the building at 1:00 a.m.

Mr. Murdock showed up in a black car, and announced, "Gillian's got a job for you, Drew, if you're interested. I have a plane waiting to take you to D.C., but you'll need to leave now."

"Give me a minute, Mark. I'll be right with you."

Mark got back in the car and shut the door.

Drew turned to Allie. "I won't see you again, will I?" asked Allie.

Drew stared at her, memorizing her features, especially her lit-from-her-soul smile. Deep inside his chest he felt a tight, hard pain. "I'm sorry, Allie."

Her gaze ripped over him, hiding nothing of her emotions. She backed away a few steps. The driver of the car beeped his horn.

She wouldn't take her eyes off him. She wasn't going to make any of this easy. "Take care of yourself, Tinkerbell."

Drew turned to get into the car, one hand gripping the frame. He closed his eyes briefly, wanting more and knowing it wasn't possible. Keep moving. Somehow those words just seemed so hollow. He started to climb in.

He felt a warm hand on his shoulder and when he turned, she was there against him, her hand sliding up his chest, her fingers at his nape and pulling him down to her.

Her mouth covered his and Drew trapped her against him, his entire body igniting like a rocket. He felt that crackling current between them. Intoxicating, leaving him useless and hungering for more.

Abruptly, she pulled away and moved out of his arms. Drew felt suddenly stripped, empty. Then she walked across the street toward the waiting car that would take her home, never once looking back.

Drew watched her go.

15

HE STOOD by her bed in the dim room. She was checking out today. She slept peacefully. His heart wrenched in his chest at the thought of losing her. Her sister had lied to him, but he couldn't blame her. It had taken him some time, but he'd found out that Gina had been transferred to Walter Reed Hospital.

He'd made sure that Gina's sister would have a chance to get out of that buy alive. He'd jury-rigged a phone to send a taped message to the FBI. Miyagi was dead; both women were free from that threat.

He wanted to tell her so she could understand. He couldn't have her, couldn't care, because they were both balanced on a knife point and because everything he ever wanted was ripped away from him in the end anyway. He didn't need the pain, didn't think he could stand it. He could never say any of those things. It had to be a quiet goodbye.

All he could think was that he wanted to hold her. Just for a while. Just for what was left of the night. He wanted to hold her and kiss her, and find some comfort.

It wasn't as if he didn't need her....

Longing welled inside him, and he reached out to touch her, to ease the ache, to fill the hole in his heart if only temporarily. He touched her cheek, revelling anew at the softness of it. He leaned down and sampled her lips, soft in her drugged sleep, drinking in the taste more soothing than wine. His palms framed her face. He drank again of her sweetness, his lips trembling on hers.

"Jammer," she murmured.

He shushed her and she settled deeper into a healing sleep.

Then he gave in to what he needed. He pressed into her and held her to him. His heart beat a painful cannonade against the wall of his chest.

He held her until he felt the sun rise, then he let her go.

Outside, much later, he watched her walking out of the hospital with her men surrounding her. Watched her get into a car and drive away. He looked up at the morning sky smudged with the first light of dawn. He wanted to love her. His heart ached for it so, it nearly took his breath. It surprised him after all this time, after all the hard lessons, that he could still be vulnerable. He should have been able to steel himself against it. He should have known enough to turn her away. Yet he had wanted so badly just to touch her, just to know she was okay.

He had wanted her from the first. Desire he understood. It was simple, basic, elemental. But this…this was something he could never be trusted with again. And because he knew that, he had somehow believed he would never be tempted. Now he felt like a jerk, betrayed by his own heart, and he kicked himself mercilessly for it. Stupid, selfish bastard…. He couldn't allow himself to fall in love with Gina Callahan.

She deserved far better than him.

HOW MANY MORE stinking swamps could this country have, Drew thought as he trudged through more saw grass and standing water. Frost was behind him with an unconscious female DEA agent across his back in a fireman's carry and bringing up the rear was Leila.

They had just rescued this agent from some hole Eduardo Fuentes had dug in his compound and called a prison. Drew smiled, remembering the huge explosion that had been a great distraction in rescuing the agent. While the narco-terrorists were running willy-nilly due to Leila's covering fire, Drew had gotten the woman out.

Now all they had to do was get to their evacuation point and they were home-free.

Not a minute went past that Drew didn't remember his goodbye to Allie. His regrets twisted him up inside.

A bullet plunked into the water in front of him and Drew yelled, "Get to cover."

Leila turned and started to return fire as all three of them ran for the forest. They were very close to the rendezvous point where the chopper would meet them to fly them out of here.

Frost pushed the unconscious agent at Drew. "Get her out. I can hear the chopper. Leila and I will cover you."

Then he was gone, disappearing into the foliage.

Drew hefted the woman across his back and started running. He was steps away from the chopper when one of Fuentes's goons came out of the jungle pointing a gun right at him.

Drew froze. He was a dead man.

Then the guy folded to the ground and the way was clear. Drew only caught a glimpse of Frost as he moved away. Breathing hard, he slung the DEA agent into the arms of the men standing in the open chopper door.

He turned to help Frost and Leila, but saw they were already hotfooting it to the helicopter. He laid down covering fire as they jumped to safety. The chopper took off.

Drew leaned back, and, for a moment, he met Frost's eyes. He didn't say a word, but Frost nodded as if he saved Drew's life every day.

It was then and there that Drew accepted, finally accepted, that these members of his team were his friends, along with Thad and Jason. He'd been a fool to turn away from Allie, a fool to fear his own emotions. Allie had been right. He *could* change his life. He was the only one who could change his life. He loved her and as soon as he got back to LA, he was going to tell her so.

ALLIE STOOD in Lily Walden's living room.

"Do you agree with me, Allie? The color just isn't right."

"It isn't. I agree. I brought a bunch of throw pillows, I'll get it right. I promise."

"I've got to go out. I'll see you later." Lily left the room and Allie heard the door open and close.

Throw pillows weren't exactly what Allie wanted to think about at the moment. Callie was awake and she was coming home today! She and Max were going to meet her at LAX this afternoon.

It probably meant a trip out to Covina to visit the family, but Allie didn't mind. In fact, she was looking forward to it. No longer would she feel like a ditz. Drew had helped her see that what she had to offer, in her own way, had merit. She didn't have to hide herself in her sister's shadow anymore. She'd performed for her country, and, although they hadn't caught the Ghost, she'd helped to get rid of a terrible threat to her sister's life.

It still hurt to think of Drew, but it had only been three days since she'd last seen him. Still, three days was too many. She prayed once again for his safe return from whatever mission Mr. Murdock had sent him on. She would never forget him and the impact he'd made on her life.

She sighed and got back to the business at hand.

Allie bent down and dumped out what she'd brought. She had pumpkin and coral. More pink or more orange. Hmm. She thought either one would go. She decided to flip them in the air and the one that touched down first would be her choice.

She threw them and turned. Drew stood there with a coral pillow in his hands. "Okay, so maybe you're not as happy to see me as I thought you'd be."

"Drew!" Allie shrieked and ran into his arms. "Ohmigod! I didn't think... I thought... You're here."

He laughed, but it was cut off. Allie laid her mouth none too gently over his. She was taken with his intoxicating scent of hard, hot male, and the connection that sizzled between them the moment she'd touched him.

His lips lingered over hers. "I love you, Allie."

He loved her. The mere thought made her chest tighten and her pulse race.

Her eyes popped open. "I love you, too. So much." Suddenly she noticed the scrape on his face. "What happened? You've been hurt."

"A mission I can't talk about. Don't look so worried. I've decided that I want to spend more time with you, rather than traipsing all over the world getting my butt into hot water. I've accepted a position with Watchdog to train their new recruits and I'll have my hands full as Frost, Leila, Jason and Thad have all been hired by them. The director was very pleased with our performance and made them all an offer they couldn't refuse."

"That's amazing. So now I don't have to worry about you in danger every day. Can't say I'm sorry about that, but you'll always be my secret agent. And you'll always be the man who showed me that I can accomplish what I set out to do, even when it gets hard." Allie smiled.

"You showed me that I don't have to give up what I want anymore. I've never followed through with anything and you've had to give up everything that meant anything to you. We've both learned that we can change and grow. We can do more together than we could alone."

"In the past, it's been safer to walk away, but not this time," Drew acknowledged.

"No, not this time, Drew. This time we both stick."

"Just think, this all started because I found you in the wrong bed."

"Mmm, and I was the wrong sister."

"At the wrong time."

"But, I found you, my oh-so-right man."

"Looks like we're in the right place now and I have the right sister in my arms. I'm never letting you go."

"I'm never letting you go, either, Drew. And you're sure about loving me?"

"Yes, Allie." He chuckled. I'm taking your advice and going after those unknown demons. Change can be very scary."

"Demons, huh? More Lake of Fire stuff. That is scary. Can I come?"

"It could be dangerous."

"I've faced danger before. I laugh in the face of danger. Ha. So, can I come?"

"I came here betting on it, Tinkerbell."

Epilogue

"SHE'S PROBABLY going to marry him, Max. You'd better get used to the idea," Callie Carpenter said to her scowling brother.

"He better make her happy."

"He's not doing missions anymore. Allie says he'll be training."

"Well, that'll allow her to sleep at night." He didn't like the shadows under Callie's eyes or the gaunt look of her. "You need more rest. Why don't you turn in?"

"I will, but I'm not done with this Ghost mission, Max. Not by a long shot."

"Why do you think the Ghost called the FBI? It couldn't have been in his best interests to get us involved."

"I don't know, Max. I'll ask him when I arrest him."

Max had no doubt that she would. He rose when she did and hugged her tightly to him. Max had got into the FBI to make the world safe for the one thing in this life that made it worth living. His family. The fact that his sister chose to go into black ops was something he was totally against, but he was thankful that she was alive and that Miyagi hadn't got his hands on her. If the man wasn't dead already, Max would have taken him out.

But the Ghost was just as big a threat. He'd been doing

what he wanted for too long. It was time for him to really get ghosted.

"I'll catch him, Max. I promise."

He watched her walk to his guest room. She was going back home in the morning to recover under his mother's excellent care. His parents knew nothing about Callie's real job and, of course, it had to stay that way.

"Not if I get to him first," Max warned. He hadn't been top in his class at Quantico for nothing. "He's going down and he's going down hard."

Or he'd die trying.

* * * * *

*Celebrate 60 years of pure reading pleasure
with Harlequin®!
Silhouette® Romantic Suspense is celebrating
with the glamour-filled, adrenaline-charged series*
LOVE IN 60 SECONDS
*starting in April 2009.
Six stories that promise to bring the glitz
of Las Vegas, the danger of revenge, the mystery
of a missing diamond, family scandals and
ripped-from-the-headlines intrigue.
Get your heart racing as love happens in sixty seconds!
Enjoy a sneak peek of*
USA TODAY *bestselling author
Marie Ferrarella's*
THE HEIRESS'S 2-WEEK AFFAIR.
*Available April 2009 from
Silhouette® Romantic Suspense.*

Eight years ago Matt Shaffer had vanished out of Natalie Rothchild's life, leaving behind a one-line note tucked under a pillow that had grown cold: *I'm sorry, but this just isn't going to work.*

That was it. No explanation, no real indication of remorse. The note had been as clinical and compassionless as an eviction notice, which, in effect, it had been, Natalie thought as she navigated through the morning traffic. Matt had written the note to evict her from his life.

She'd spent the next two weeks crying, breaking down without warning as she walked down the street, or as she sat staring at a meal she couldn't bring herself to eat.

Candace, she remembered with a bittersweet pang, had tried to get her to go clubbing in order to get her to forget about Matt.

She'd turned her twin down, but she did get her act together. If Matt didn't think enough of their relationship to try to contact her, to try to make her understand why he'd changed so radically from lover to stranger, then to hell with him. He was dead to her, she resolved. And he'd remained that way.

Until twenty minutes ago.

The adrenaline in her veins kept mounting.

Natalie focused on her driving. Vegas in the daylight wasn't nearly as alluring, as magical and glitzy as it was after dark. Like an aging woman best seen in soft lighting, Vegas's imperfections were all visible in the daylight. Natalie supposed that was why people like her sister didn't like to get up until noon. They lived for the night.

Except that Candace could no longer do that.

The thought brought a fresh, sharp ache with it.

"Dammit, Candy, what a waste," Natalie murmured under her breath.

She pulled up before the Janus casino. One of the three valets currently on duty came to life and made a beeline for her vehicle.

"Welcome to the Janus," the young attendant said cheerfully as he opened her door with a flourish.

"We'll see," she replied solemnly.

As he pulled away with her car, Natalie looked up at the casino's logo. Janus was the Roman god with two faces, one pointed toward the past, the other facing the future. It struck her as rather ironic, given what she was doing here, seeking out someone from her past in order to get answers so that the future could be settled.

The moment she entered the casino, the Vegas phenomena took hold. It was like stepping into a world where time did not matter or even make an appearance. There was only a sense of "now."

Because in Natalie's experience she'd discovered that bartenders knew the inner workings of any establishment they worked for better than anyone else, she made her way to the first bar she saw within the casino.

The bartender in attendance was a gregarious man in his early forties. He had a quick, sexy smile, which was probably one of the main reasons he'd been hired. His name tag identified him as Kevin.

Moving to her end of the bar, Kevin asked, "What'll it be, pretty lady?"

"Information." She saw a dubious look cross his brow. To counter that, she took out her badge. Granted she wasn't here in an official capacity, but Kevin didn't need to know that. "Were you on duty last night?"

Kevin began to wipe the gleaming black surface of the bar. "You mean, during the gala?"

"Yes."

The smile gracing his lips was a satisfied one. Last night had obviously been profitable for him, she judged. "I caught an extra shift."

She took out Candace's photograph and carefully placed it on the bar. "Did you happen to see this woman there?"

The bartender glanced at the picture. Mild interest turned to recognition. "You mean, Candace Rothchild? Yeah, she was here, as loud and brassy as always. But not for long," he added, looking rather disappointed. There was always a circus when Candace was around, Natalie thought. "She and the boss had at it and then he had our head of security escort her out."

She latched on to the first part of his statement. "They argued? About what?"

He shook his head. "Couldn't tell you. Too far away for anything but body language," he confessed.

"And the head of security?" she asked.

"He got her to leave."

She leaned in over the bar. "Tell me about him."

"Don't know much," the bartender admitted. "Just that

his name's Matt Shaffer. Boss flew him in from L.A., where he was head of security for Montgomery Enterprises."

There was no avoiding it, she thought darkly. She was going to have to talk to Matt. The thought left her cold. "Do you know where I can find him right now?"

Kevin glanced at his watch. "He should be in his office. On the second floor, toward the rear." He gave her the numbers of the rooms where the monitors that kept watch over the casino guests as they tried their luck against the house were located.

Taking out a twenty, she placed it on the bar. "Thanks for your help."

Kevin slipped the bill into his vest pocket. "Anytime, lovely lady," he called after her. "Anytime."

She debated going up the stairs, then decided on the elevator. The car that took her up to the second floor was empty. Natalie stepped out of the elevator, looked around to get her bearings and then walked toward the rear of the floor.

"Into the Valley of Death rode the six hundred," she silently recited, digging deep for a line from a poem by Tennyson. Wrapping her hand around a brass handle, she opened one of the glass doors and walked in.

The woman whose desk was closest to the door looked up. "You can't come in here. This is a restricted area."

Natalie already had her ID in her hand and held it up. "I'm looking for Matt Shaffer," she told the woman.

God, even saying his name made her mouth go dry. She was supposed to be over him, to have moved on with her life. What happened?

The woman began to answer her. "He's—"

"Right here."

The deep voice came from behind her. Natalie felt every single nerve ending go on tactical alert at the same moment that all the hairs at the back of her neck stood up. Eight years had passed, but she would have recognized his voice anywhere.

* * * * *

Why did Matt Shaffer leave
heiress-turned-cop Natalie Rothchild?
What does he know about the
death of Natalie's twin sister?
Come and meet these two reunited lovers
and learn the secrets of the Rothchild family in
THE HEIRESS'S 2-WEEK AFFAIR
by USA TODAY *bestselling author*
Marie Ferrarella.
The first book in
Silhouette® Romantic Suspense's
wildly romantic new continuity,
LOVE IN 60 SECONDS!
Available April 2009.

CELEBRATE
60 YEARS
OF PURE READING PLEASURE
WITH **HARLEQUIN**®!

Look for Silhouette®
Romantic Suspense in April!

Love In 60 Seconds
Bright lights. Big city. Hearts in overdrive.

Silhouette® Romantic Suspense is celebrating Harlequin's 60th Anniversary with six stories that promise to bring readers the glitz of Las Vegas, the danger of revenge, the mystery of a missing diamond, and family scandals.

**Look for the first title, *The Heiress's 2-Week Affair*
by *USA TODAY* bestselling author
Marie Ferrarella, on sale in April!**

His 7-Day Fiancée by **Gail Barrett**	May
The 9-Month Bodyguard by **Cindy Dees**	June
Prince Charming for 1 Night by **Nina Bruhns**	July
Her 24-Hour Protector by **Loreth Anne White**	August
5 minutes to Marriage by **Carla Cassidy**	September

You're invited to join our Tell Harlequin Reader Panel!

By joining our new reader panel you will:

- Receive Harlequin® books—they are FREE and yours to keep with no obligation to purchase anything!
- Participate in fun online surveys
- Exchange opinions and ideas with women just like you
- Have a say in our new book ideas and help us publish the best in women's fiction

In addition, you will have a chance to win great prizes and receive special gifts!
See Web site for details. Some conditions apply.
Space is limited.

To join, visit us at

www.TellHarlequin.com.

The Inside Romance newsletter has a NEW look for the new year!

Same great content, brand-new look!

The Inside Romance newsletter is a FREE quarterly newsletter highlighting our upcoming series releases and promotions!

Click on the Inside Romance link on the front page of
www.eHarlequin.com or e-mail us at
insideromance@harlequin.ca to sign up
to receive your FREE newsletter today!

You can also subscribe by writing to us at: HARLEQUIN BOOKS
Attention: Customer Service Department
P.O. Box 9057, Buffalo, NY 14269-9057

Please allow 4-6 weeks for delivery of the first issue by mail.

IRNNEW09

REQUEST YOUR FREE BOOKS!

2 FREE NOVELS PLUS 2 FREE GIFTS!

HARLEQUIN®

Blaze

Red-hot reads!

YES! Please send me 2 FREE Harlequin® Blaze™ novels and my 2 FREE gifts (gifts are worth about $10). After receiving them, if I don't wish to receive any more books, I can return the shipping statement marked "cancel". If I don't cancel, I will receive 6 brand-new novels every month and be billed just $4.24 per book in the U.S. or $4.71 per book in Canada. Shipping and handling is just 25¢ per book. That's a savings of 15% or more off the cover price! I understand that accepting the 2 free books and gifts places me under no obligation to buy anything. I can always return a shipment and cancel at any time. Even if I never buy another book, the two free books and gifts are mine to keep forever.

151 HDN ERVA 351 HDN ERUX

Name	(PLEASE PRINT)	
Address		Apt. #
City	State/Prov.	Zip/Postal Code

Signature (if under 18, a parent or guardian must sign)

Mail to the **Harlequin Reader Service:**
IN U.S.A.: P.O. Box 1867, Buffalo, NY 14240-1867
IN CANADA: P.O. Box 609, Fort Erie, Ontario L2A 5X3

Not valid to current subscribers of Harlequin Blaze books.

Want to try two free books from another line?
Call 1-800-873-8635 or visit www.morefreebooks.com.

* Terms and prices subject to change without notice. Prices do not include applicable taxes. N.Y. residents add applicable sales tax. Canadian residents will be charged applicable provincial taxes and GST. Offer not valid in Quebec. This offer is limited to one order per household. All orders subject to approval. Credit or debit balances in a customer's account(s) may be offset by any other outstanding balance owed by or to the customer. Please allow 4 to 6 weeks for delivery. Offer available while quantities last.

Your Privacy: Harlequin Books is committed to protecting your privacy. Our Privacy Policy is available online at www.eHarlequin.com or upon request from the Reader Service. From time to time we make our lists of customers available to reputable third parties who may have a product or service of interest to you. If you would prefer we not share your name and address, please check here. ☐

HB09R

HARLEQUIN® *Blaze*™

Two delightfully sexy stories.
Two determined, free-spirited heroines
and two irresistible heroes...
who won't have a clue what hit them!

Don't miss
TAWNY WEBER'S
first duet:

Coming On Strong
April 2009

and

Going Down Hard
May 2009

The spring is turning out to be a hot one!

Available wherever Harlequin books are sold.

COMING NEXT MONTH

Available March 31, 2009

#459 OUT OF CONTROL Julie Miller
From 0–60
Detective Jack Riley is determined to uncover who's behind the movement of drugs through Dahlia Speedway. And he'll do whatever it takes to find out—even go undercover as a driver. But can he keep his hands off sexy mechanic Alex Morgan?

#460 NAKED ATTRACTION Jule McBride
Robby Robriquet's breathtaking looks and chiseled bod just can't be denied. But complications ensue for Ellie Lee and Robby when his dad wants Ellie's business skills for a sneaky scheme that jeopardizes their love all over again....

#461 ONCE A GAMBLER Carrie Hudson
Stolen from Time, Bk. 2
Riverboat gambler Jake Gannon's runnin', cheatin' ways may have come to an end when he aids the sweet Ellie Winslow in her search for her sister. Ellie claims she's been sent back in time, but Jake's bettin' he'll be able to convince her to stay!

#462 COMING ON STRONG Tawny Weber
Paybacks can be hell. That's what Belle Forsham finds out when she looks up former fiancé Mitch Carter. So she left him at the altar six years ago? But she needs his help now. What else can she do but show him what he's been missing?

#463 THE RIGHT STUFF Lori Wilde
Uniformly Hot!
Taylor Milton is researching her next planned fantasy adventure resort—Out of This World Lovemaking—featuring sexy air force high fliers. Volunteering for duty is Lieutenant Colonel Dr. Daniel Corben, who's ready and able to take the glam heiress to the moon and back!

#464 SHE'S GOT IT BAD Sarah Mayberry
Zoe Ford can't believe that Liam Masters has walked into her tattoo parlor. After all this time he's still an irresistible bad boy. But she's no longer sweet and innocent. And she has a score to settle with him. One that won't be paid until he's hot, bothered and begging for more.